S0-CQQ-951

"It's a man's job."

Abruptly, Cassie dropped back on her heels and…laughed.

"You didn't do that right."

"Do what right?"

"The tough male act. You need to throw out your chest more, and thrust your hip forward." Standing, she did a parody of one of her brothers. "Then you use a tough, gravelly tone of voice and say, *'it's a man's job.'*" She grinned. "Just like that."

Jake sincerely doubted any man could move like Cassie and say anything in such a throaty, breathless voice. If he did, he would be arrested for making an indecent proposal. The words didn't matter, but the body language and tone said everything. And the really hellish part about hearing Cassie do it was that she didn't seem to have any interest in him as a man.

Yet.

Dear Reader,

This month, Silhouette Romance has a wonderful lineup—
sure to add love and laughter to your sunny summer days
and sultry nights. Marie Ferrarella starts us off with another
FABULOUS FATHER in *The Women in Joe Sullivan's Life*.
Sexy Joe Sullivan was an expert on *grown* women, but when
he suddenly finds himself raising three small nieces, he needs
the help of Maggie McGuire—and finds himself falling
for her womanly charms as well as her maternal instinct!
Cassandra Cavannaugh has plans for her own BUNDLE OF
JOY in Julianna Morris's *Baby Talk*. And Jake O'Connor
had no intention of being part of them. Can true love turn
Mr. Wrong into a perfect father—and husband for Cassie?

Dorsey Kelley spins another thrilling tale for WRANGLERS
AND LACE in *Cowboy for Hire*. Bent Murray thought
his rodeo days were behind him, until sassy cowgirl
Kate Monahan forced him to face his past—and her place
in his heart. Handsome Michael Damian gets more than
he bargained for in Christine Scott's *Imitation Bride*.
Lacey Keegan was only pretending to be his fiancée, but
now that wedding plans were snowballing, he began
wishing that their make-believe romance was real.

Two more stories with humor and love round out the
month in *Second Chance at Marriage* by Pamela Dalton,
and *An Improbable Wife* by debut author Sally Carleen.

Happy Reading!

Anne Canadeo

Senior Editor, Silhouette Romance

Please address questions and book requests to:
Silhouette Reader Service
U.S.: 3010 Walden Ave., P.O. Box 1325, Buffalo, NY 14269
Canadian: P.O. Box 609, Fort Erie, Ont. L2A 5X3

BABY
TALK

Julianna Morris

Silhouette
ROMANCE™
Published by Silhouette Books
America's Publisher of Contemporary Romance

If you purchased this book without a cover you should be aware that this book is stolen property. It was reported as "unsold and destroyed" to the publisher, and neither the author nor the publisher has received any payment for this "stripped book."

To my mother and sister—for both keeping my feet on the ground and my head in the clouds.
Thanks for being there.

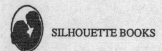 SILHOUETTE BOOKS

ISBN 0-373-19097-2

BABY TALK

Copyright © 1995 by Martha Ann Ford

All rights reserved. Except for use in any review, the reproduction or utilization of this work in whole or in part in any form by any electronic, mechanical or other means, now known or hereafter invented, including xerography, photocopying and recording, or in any information storage or retrieval system, is forbidden without the written permission of the editorial office, Silhouette Books, 300 East 42nd Street, New York, NY 10017 U.S.A.

All characters in this book have no existence outside the imagination of the author and have no relation whatsoever to anyone bearing the same name or names. They are not even distantly inspired by any individual known or unknown to the author, and all incidents are pure invention.

This edition published by arrangement with Harlequin Books S.A.

® and TM are trademarks of Harlequin Books S.A., used under license. Trademarks indicated with ® are registered in the United States Patent and Trademark Office, the Canadian Trade Marks Office and in other countries.

Printed in U.S.A.

JULIANNA MORRIS

has an offbeat sense of humor, which frequently gets her into trouble. She is often accused of being curious about everything...her interests ranging from oceanography and photography, to traveling, antiquing, walking on the beach and reading science fiction. Choosing a college major was extremely difficult, but after many changes she earned a bachelor's degree in environmental science.

Julianna's writing is supervised by a cat named Gandalf, who sits on the computer monitor and criticizes each keystroke. Ultimately, she would like a home overlooking the ocean, where she can write to her heart's content—and Gandalf's malcontent. She'd like to share that home with her own romantic hero, someone with a warm, sexy smile, lots of patience and an offbeat sense of humor to match her own. Oh, yes...and he has to like cats.

Bundles of Joy

Dear Readers,

My oldest brother made me an aunt at the ripe old age of four. I remember running through the house that June morning crying, "I'm an aunt, I'm an aunt," then stopping and confusedly asking, "What's an aunt?" Well, twelve more nephews and nieces have arrived since then to teach me.

As a child I rushed headlong into the future, anxious to become an adult. How delightful it is to look around now and celebrate those marvelous creations...babies. I have always wanted children. Like my heroine, I can hardly wait to hold my own "bundle of joy" in my arms. Children bring hope and vision into distant tomorrows. Seen through their eyes, the world is a remarkable place of magic and mystery.

Kids are overwhelming, challenging, awe inspiring, unpredictable and exhausting. I know...I've seen five brothers raising their families. They are also utterly wonderful. I'll gladly take the sleepless nights in exchange for a million smiles. I'll let the anxious moments be forgotten, swept away by childish giggles and gifts of macaroni necklaces. The spilled paint on the floor won't matter, because my son or daughter will have just created a "masterpiece." Above all, I'll take the love and hope of their creation.

Best wishes

Julieanna Mories

Chapter One

"I don't want you going to a sperm bank," Virgie declared, stabbing a fork into her salad.

Cassie sighed; if only she'd kept quiet about her plans to have a baby, then she wouldn't be having this pointless discussion. She looked at the older woman firmly. "I've made up my mind."

"But having a baby with a total stranger is so impersonal."

"I won't be having it *with* him," Cassie corrected. Her meal was suddenly unappealing, and she pushed it to one side. Virgie couldn't say anything she hadn't already thought about a hundred times. "I won't even know the father's name."

"That's even worse." Virgie leaned forward, her brown eyes full of appeal. "I've been thinking.... You know I asked my son to come by and check out the locks?"

"Yes, but what—"

"Oh, good, he's here," Virgie said, smiling. She waved her hand toward the door.

Glancing around, Cassie caught a brief impression of a tall man walking toward them. He looked absurdly out of place in the senior center, where the average male age was seventy-one years.

Virgie's voice dropped to a whisper. "Take a good look and see what you think. I haven't said anything to him yet, but maybe Jake could donate his sperm."

Taken by surprise, Cassie swallowed her coffee the wrong way and began coughing. A moment later someone passed her a glass of water, which she gulped down gratefully. She snatched a handful of napkins and wiped away her tears.

"Are you all right?" a deep voice asked.

Cassie peered over the damp napkins. Jake O'Connor crouched at the side of the table, denims stretching over a pair of muscular legs. He was strong jawed and a trifle brooding, with eyes that were intense, humorous... and a piercing green.

His hand touched her shoulder in an impersonal way, but to Cassie's chagrin her body flared to instant attention. "I—" she started to say, then stopped abruptly. *Oh, great. He hadn't heard his mother's suggestion, had he?*

"Ma'am?"

"I'm fine," she muttered. She straightened, tossed the crumpled napkins onto the table and tried to regain her tattered dignity. "I'm terrific."

"'Course she's fine," Virgie announced.

Jake smiled kindly and patted Cassie's arm. She gritted her teeth and began to dislike him. He'd clearly classified her with stray kittens, little old ladies and feminine wallflowers.

Virgie tugged on Jake's collar. "Come on, give your old mother a kiss," she ordered.

He rose, dwarfing her. "Old?" His dark eyebrows lifted. "Why, you don't look a day over sixty."

"Watch your mouth."

In addition to a kiss, he gave her a massive bear hug that had Virgie declaring she couldn't breathe. But from her glowing expression Cassie didn't think she minded.

So this was Jake: Jake the wonderful, Jake the perfect. He was tall and broad-shouldered enough to make her feel delicate, even though she was a generous five foot eight inches in her bare feet. Men like Jake were attracted to voluptuous, confident, honey-skinned women, not to quiet, unassuming directors of community senior centers.

"Cassie darling, meet my son," Virgie said when Jake released her. "Let me know what you think." She winked.

Cassie's eyes widened. What did she think? She thought Virgie was out of her mind! "Forget it," she ordered.

"But—"

"No. Absolutely not."

"What's going on?" Jake asked, watching the emotions flutter across the faces of the two women. He knew his mother; she had something up her sleeve, and he hoped it wasn't another attempt at matchmaking.

Not that this new victim wasn't nice. She was pretty—in a rather understated way—and she had a generous, beautifully shaped mouth. He liked her mouth. In fact, he liked it quite a lot. And he liked the way she held her composure, with no checking her appearance or fluttering with false coyness.

"Female stuff is going on," Virgie told him. "I told you about Cassie Cavannaugh—she's the director of the senior center. She's also going to be my new tenant. That's why I asked you to repair that deck behind the cottage."

It was worse than Jake had thought. His mother was moving in for the kill. The "cottage" was located just fifty feet from the main house; he'd stumble over this newest prospect every time he came for a visit.

He glanced at Cassie again, trying to see what was so special about the lady. She had that wholesome, small-town look. Well-scrubbed, minimum makeup, a delicate, heart-shaped face surrounded by a heavy sweep of gold hair and stormy gray-blue eyes that were both direct and enigmatic at the same time. *Not bad*. Not his type, but definitely not bad.

Damnation.

It wasn't that he had anything against marriage, at least not for other people. Unfortunately his brief attempt at marital bliss had been the biggest disaster of his life. Jake wasn't cut out for love and domesticity; it was as simple as that.

A pair of fingers snapped in front of his face.

He blinked. "What?"

"Wake up, son. I want you to make a good impression on Cassie."

Jake looked at the young woman and smiled weakly. "It's...uh...nice meeting you." He watched the color shift in her eyes, becoming a cool silver, and knew she recognized the lack of sincerity in his voice.

"Actually this isn't the first time you two have met," his mother added.

Hell. Jake searched his mind yet couldn't recall ever seeing Cassie Cavannaugh before in his life. "Really?"

"You were in high school together."

"That was a long time ago," Cassie said quietly. "I think I remember, but then he's much older. I could be thinking of someone else."

Her comment made Jake feel ancient, then he detected a hint of mischief in her face. Interesting. "I can't be that much older. When did you grad—"

"Now, now," Virgie interrupted. "You'll have plenty of time to compare notes. You promised you'd stay for a month."

Jake barely controlled his groan. He should have known better than to make that promise, but he'd needed a rest, somewhere quiet and without the high-tech pressures of his work as a security consultant.

"Son?" Virgie prompted.

"Right," he said, wishing he sounded more gracious. Jake loved his mother—she was impossible and funny and often totally absurd. They didn't see enough of each other because his work carried him all over the world, and she didn't like to travel. "A month," he reluctantly repeated.

"Well, then, you'll have lots of time to visit with Cassie."

"Mother," he warned, but she just gave him an innocent smile. "I'm going to be busy."

"I know," Virgie protested. "You've got all that work to do at the house, especially on the cottage. That's why we're so grateful you offered to check things out over here, as well."

Offered? Jake almost laughed. He'd been ordered to come to the senior center. His instincts for self-preservation must have malfunctioned, but a senior center had seemed innocuous enough. Who would have guessed the director was a sweet-faced bit of marriage bait?

His next thought collided with the word *we're. We're* so grateful you offered... was that the universal *we,* or did it mean Cassie Cavannaugh specifically? He could only hope Cassie was as guileless as she appeared, because he hated the idea of running from the both of them.

"Ahem," Jake cleared his throat. "Is there something I should check particularly? I mean, the locks and things?"

Cassie jumped when Virgie poked a finger in her back. "Uh...you might check the back door," she said. "We had a break-in last month, and I don't think the locksmith fixed it correctly."

Jake immediately hurried to the door in question, aware that his mom was hustling her "new tenant" right along behind him. He examined the lock and pretended not to notice their presence. His fingers worked at the contrivance, testing the simple mechanics with the same intensity he devoted to more complex security devices. Finally he straightened and looked at his small audience. "I'll have to put in a new one."

His mother smiled and Cassie bit down on her lip. Jake found himself wanting to smooth the small marks left by her teeth—and then decided his head should be examined. Miss Cavannaugh was off-limits. Period.

"We'll pay for any repairs," she said in her soft voice. "Tell me what you need, and I'll go to the hardware store."

"That's not necessary," Jake said immediately. "I'll go myself. I should be able to fix everything today."

Virgie frowned thoughtfully. "Will you have time?" she asked. "Remember, you're expected at the park later."

"Yeah, right," he growled. His mother had conned him into playing referee for a junior soccer game, on his first day of vacation no less!

"Good. We'll see you later, then. Cassie is one of the team coaches."

Hook, line and sinker. His mother ranked with the best matchmakers of all time. Only it wasn't going to work. No way. "Aren't those boys' teams?" Jake asked automatically.

"So?" asked Cassie coolly.

"Well, I just thought the boys would probably have a guy coach...you know."

Her chin lifted, and anger deepened the color in her cheeks. "No, I don't know. The 'boys' just want to play, and I'm the best coach they've had for a long time."

"Why doesn't one of the fathers do it?"

"Nobody had time. Besides, everyone is thrilled I took over. *Including* the team."

Jake opened his mouth, then closed it quickly. "I didn't mean..." *Hell's bells,* what did he mean? His mother's matchmaking had rattled his brain. "Never mind. I'll get that lock. See you later, Mom."

He practically broke the speed of light getting to the door, and it wasn't until he was sitting in his car that he realized how rude he must have appeared—but better rude than "sized" up as a prospective husband.

* * *

As soon as they were alone, Virgie smiled happily. "You must see what a great sperm donor Jake would be," she said, ignoring Cassie's attempts to silence her. "He's strong and healthy. He had the normal childhood diseases, but nothing major. He's handsome...he gets that from *my* side of the family—and he practices safe sex."

If Cassie had been uncomfortable before, now she was ready to jump into a volcano at the first scream for a sacrificial virgin. Not that she was a virgin any longer, but it had been a while, so she was the closest Sandpiper Cove, Oregon, had to such a thing.

Yet she felt a morbid curiosity. "How do you know?"

"Know what?"

"That he practices safe sex."

"Oh." Virgie waved her hands in a pooh-poohing motion. "Easy. He has scads of condoms around his apartment whenever I go for a visit."

Cassie doubted that even Jake was arrogant enough to keep condoms in plain view, especially with a visiting parent. "Just around?" she asked, skeptical.

"Well, yes. You know...here and there."

"Here and there. Perhaps concealed in the nightstand by his bed, where no self-respecting mother has the right to be snooping?"

Virgie didn't seem the least disconcerted. "*All* self-respecting mothers snoop. It's a skill you'll have to learn. Besides, I wasn't snooping, I was exploring."

"Uh-huh."

"He was such an adorable boy. I wish I had my photo album with me."

Cassie had seen the photo album *numerous* times, and there was no doubt Jake had been adorable. The baby in those pictures was a mischievous imp with an intelligent, merry face. He'd grown up into a very pleasant male package—one who didn't like small towns and preferred the fast pace of city life, according to his mother.

"Virgie, I...er...appreciate what you're trying to do, but—"

"He's perfect for this."

"Perfect for what?"

They looked around and saw Phyllis Mulvey standing nearby, her eyes wide and curious. Cassie groaned. Phyllis was the worst gossip at the center. If someone wanted everyone to know something, they made sure she heard it first. She was the updated version of the town crier and she took her role seriously.

"Cassie wants—"

"It's nothing," Cassie interrupted. She gave Virgie a look of dire warning. Phyllis's gaze flashed back and forth between them. She was a nice lady, but Cassie doubted she was ready to be shocked out of her support stockings.

"You can't keep it a secret forever," Virgie said reasonably.

"That doesn't mean I need to announce my plans to the whole world," Cassie explained, exasperated.

"Rubbish," Virgie said dismissively. "It's very simple. Cassie wants to have a baby. And I don't see why she has to go to some sperm bank when I have a perfectly good, healthy son who can donate for her. Besides, how else am I going to get to be a grandmother?" she wailed.

By now they had a small audience crowding around them, and a murmur of discussion arose. Phyllis stared, her eyes wide. All at once she patted her blue-tinted white hair and squared her shoulders. "I think that's a selfish thing to do, Virginia O'Connor...trying to sneak your son in when the rest of us were in the dark. I have a son who would make a great father."

"You already have six grandchildren," Virgie snapped. She was wearing a bulldog, no-one's-gonna-move-in-on-my-territory expression.

"Of all the nerve!" Lavinia Hofstad said, furious. "It doesn't matter how many grandchildren any of us have."

"Of course *you* would say that, you have more than any of us," Phyllis sniffed.

"Pooh! Your sons are all too short. Cassie doesn't want a short baby," Virgie interjected. "My Jake is perfect. Besides, I'd be the ideal grandmother. I wouldn't interfere in the slightest."

"Are you saying I interfere?" Phyllis shrieked. "I'm a much better grandparent than you would be! Why, you can't even cook."

"That has nothing to do with anything."

Cassie stared at the arguing women; the last thing she'd expected was acceptance of her plan. True, several ladies on the fringe of the discussion looked shocked—even horrified. But the leaders were in complete support of her plan; dissenters wouldn't have a chance against Virgie and friends.

Why had she confided her plans to have a baby?

You were just testing yourself.

A grimace crossed her delicate features. She'd wanted to confide in her sister-in-law, but Lisa was due to have her own baby any day, and Cassie hadn't wanted to upset her. That left Virgie, who was the most likely to understand. Still... to suggest her son as a possible sperm donor? Cassie was going to suffer acute embarrassment if he ever learned of his mother's suggestion. Sure, Jake would be a great biological father, but she couldn't imagine his going along with the idea.

Virgie was right; she couldn't have kept her secret for very long, especially after she got pregnant. *Pregnant*. Her mind worked the word, even as her lips moved silently. There was a small twinge at the base of her stomach, a combination of nerves and anticipation.

For years she'd wanted to fall in love and start a family. But it hadn't happened, and here she was, thirty-four years old and tired of looking for Mr. White Knight. Besides, how many knights did a woman meet in Sandpiper Cove? The answer was zero. To date, she had yet to meet anyone even remotely acceptable. And certainly no white knights.

"Cassie?"

She looked up to see Virgie, sitting across from her with an expression that was both concerned and aggressive. "Yes?"

"What do you think? Which one is going to be the father?"

A bevy of faces peered down, waiting anxiously for an answer. She sighed, wishing she could have let everyone believe she'd had a brief, passionate affair that hadn't worked out. It would have been much simpler.

"I don't think . . . that is, I think it would be better to go with my original plan," Cassie said slowly, watching disappointment cloud their eyes. "I'm supposed to call them . . . in two or three weeks when . . . uh . . ." Her voice trailed off. How could she explain that she was supposed to rush to Portland at the optimum time so some doctor could get her pregnant in the new, modern way, instead of the traditional way? Some things were meant to be private.

"It's really nice of all of you," she continued. "But I think an anonymous donor is best."

Phyllis offered a reassuring smile. "Don't fret, we're all behind you. It's just that it would be nice to have another grandchild." She paused and gave Virgie a stern glare. "And don't you go working on Cassie when our backs are turned."

Virgie sniffed.

All at once Cassie was tempted to laugh. She hadn't expected such unusual support from the seniors. Deciding had been so difficult because of all the things to worry about: single-motherhood, money, her job, her family. For a moment Cassie's lungs refused to work. Her two arrogant, macho brothers were going to hit the roof when she told them. Maybe she could just wait until the baby was . . . say . . . eighteen?

She was vaguely aware that Virgie was ordering everyone away from their table. They went reluctantly. Cassie was a surrogate daughter, and they felt they had the privilege of parents to advise, comfort and scold.

"I'm sorry," Virgie apologized when they no longer had an audience. "It just seemed better to let it all out so there wouldn't be a lot of foolish gossip."

"That's okay," Cassie replied with a shrug.

The older woman's bright eyes gazed at her. "I'll set up the bridge tables. I think the natives are getting restless."

"Thanks. That would help."

Virgie squeezed her hand, then left. In short order she could be heard organizing her cohorts into a work group. Cassie waited a moment, then got up and walked to her office. She spun in her desk chair and stared through the window at the small bay. Fishing boats lined the docks, interspersed with the occasional pleasure craft. It was a picturesque scene, one she'd sketched and painted several times. Each day the view was different yet the same.

In spring and summer, tourists walked along the shore and out to the docks, eating ice cream and laughing while raucous sea gulls circled overhead. In fall there were fewer people, and the sailboats were battened down for the coming winter. Each season had its own special flavor, but there was always the constancy of the ocean's presence, filling the air with the scent of salt and seaweed, defining the pace of life.

It was a life Jake O'Connor had rejected.

Cassie sighed and drew a sea gull on the desk blotter. Actually she did have a remote memory of Jake from childhood; she'd been a freshman in high school when he was a senior. The lanky teenager with an engaging grin had turned into pure, heart-stopping hunk.

A few minutes later she heard a knock, and the subject of her thoughts filled the open doorway. Taking a deep breath, Cassie told herself that Jake O'Connor was probably an insensitive jerk, even if he did make her libido sit up and take notice. "Yes?"

He hesitated before entering. "Mom asked me to check your office."

"Oh, well, go ahead. Thanks."

Bending over some papers on the desk, Cassie pretended to be engrossed in their contents, all the while watching Jake as he examined the locks on her two windows. It was all she could do to keep her mouth from watering. He had the look of someone completely comfortable within his own body. Distracted, Cassie bumped her coffee cup and sent it crashing to the floor. Jake jerked and let out a curse.

"Sorry," she apologized. She leaned down to pick up the cup, which had miraculously escaped injury.

"Not at all," he said politely. "I was finished anyway. Your windows are fine. I'll see you later...at the park."

Cassie's eyes narrowed as he vanished through the door. He didn't sound too pleased that he'd be seeing her at the soccer game, which was just too bad. If the team parents didn't object to a female coach, then it was none of his business. Just then the sound of raised voices came from the recreation room, and she listened for a moment, trying to decide if she should intervene.

"—not going to be my partner again, Phyllis doesn't know how to bid."

"Hush now, you don't..." Virgie's voice cut across the argument, then dropped to a murmur in her role as peacemaker. Cassie could imagine pointed glances and gestures in the direction of her office.

You don't want to upset Cassie.

Oh, no, Virgie wouldn't want to upset her. She still hoped to convince Cassie that Jake was an ideal sperm donor. Actually it was a unique approach to becoming a grandmother, but unique and possible weren't the same.

Pressing her hand to her abdomen, Cassie tried to imagine a baby growing there. "Soon," she whispered.

A delighted smile grew on her face. Except for the embarrassment, it would have been priceless to see Jake's expression when his mother made her "proposal."

Utterly priceless.

Chapter Two

Cassie waved goodbye to the seniors lingering by their cars, then hurried to her own vehicle and sped away. Her stomach was growling, a reminder she hadn't eaten much lunch. At her apartment she raced between packed boxes, scrambling to pull on different clothes while gulping down a peanut-butter-and-jelly sandwich. By her calculations she had a half hour to get ready and get to the park for the game.

When she passed the mirror she did a double take, then grimaced; the most she could say for her appearance was that she looked youthful. Caught in a high ponytail, her hair was the ultimate lack of sophistication. Baggy sweatpants and a team jacket completely concealed her feminine curves, and an ancient pair of high-top sneakers dominated the whole picture. Cassie threw the crust of her sandwich at the reflection.

Drat Jake and drat his mother. Never before had she worried about how she looked at a soccer game. After all, you couldn't come dressed as a fashion plate when you were coaching an energetic bunch of boys. It would be ridiculous. She reached out with her left forefinger and wiped a faint smear of jelly from the mirror. Of course, she thought wistfully, some women looked gorgeous no matter what they were wearing.

All at once Cassie wrinkled her nose and tossed the end of her ponytail over her shoulder. Who cared if she wasn't a fashion plate? Jake O'Connor didn't count, no matter how sexy he was.

Though she drove as quickly as possible, Cassie was still a few minutes late arriving at the field. The members of the team descended on the car en masse.

"Jeez, I told you she'd get here in time," said a freckle-faced youngster. He looked at his teammates in triumph.

"Did not."

"Did too!"

Cassie cleared her throat. "Billy, David, that's enough."

The argument ended as quickly as it began. They all knew the rules about fighting and strong language, and it didn't take much of a reminder to stop an altercation.

"Need any help?"

Glancing up, Cassie encountered Jake O'Connor's green eyes. He was even more attractive than she'd thought before, and a heavy, warm sensation shot from her toes to the top of her head, lingering at the base of her stomach. *Cripes*. Men like that ought to be outlawed, especially at kids' soccer games. They could make you forget all kinds of important things.

After a moment Cassie reminded herself that, while Jake was a nice hunk of man, he was also an annoyance. Her shoulders lifted. "No, thanks. The boys were just going to do some warm-up exercises. Right, guys?"

"Right!" they chorused, setting up a line.

"Looks like you run a tight ship," Jake murmured.

"For a woman, you mean," Cassie couldn't resist saying. It didn't seem to matter that she should feel grateful for his help at the center. Over the years she'd dealt with all kinds of nonsense from her brothers; she didn't have to tolerate it from a stranger.

Jake winced. Her tone was definitely unfriendly—and for the sake of an amicable game, he'd better make peace. "Look uh . . . that's not what I meant."

"Really?" Cassie grabbed a box from the car and stomped away. Jake's breath whistled through his teeth. He preferred skimpy shorts that showed off a woman's legs, but the fabric of her sweats clung nicely to her firm, round bottom.

"Hey, Mr. Referee, you mad at our coach?"

Turning, he saw one of the boys watching him. "What?"

"Are you mad at Coach Cassie?"

"Can it, David," one of the other boys called before Jake could answer.

"But he's the referee. The ref shouldn't be mad at the coach, at least not before she calls him an idiot."

Jake felt the beginnings of a headache. "I'm not mad at Miss Cavannaugh," he assured, but the kid's freckled nose wrinkled.

"You were looking at her kind of funny, like she had bubble gum on her pants or something."

Damn. Jake's face went hot; kids were far too observant. "Aren't you supposed to be doing something? All of you?"

"Okay, okay. Jeez."

The group started doing jumping jacks, and Jake hurried to a safer location. He supposed children were okay, but a little exposure went a long way. Bubble gum? A grin crossed his face; thank goodness the youngster was too young to understand the real reason he'd been staring at Cassie Cavannaugh's rear end.

Two hours later he was ready to drop in his tracks. Coach Cassie had shed her demure exterior and turned into an energetic fireball, encouraging her team and sassing the other coach in a friendly, teasing way. She didn't look much older than the kids, especially with her ponytail pulled out the back of a baseball cap and grass stains on her knees.

The only person not included in her pleasant banter was Jake himself. She addressed him in a chilly, formal tone of voice, a sharp contrast to the camaraderie everyone else shared. Frustrated, Jake finally made a questionable call and saw her stalking toward him. He grinned.

"Are you blind? The ball wasn't out of bounds."

"I'm the referee."

"You're a jerk."

"Shame on you, Coach Cassie. I thought you only called the ref an idiot."

Her teeth gritted. It was silly to object; unless a miracle happened for the other team, the Sea Avengers were certain of winning. Jake's call wouldn't make the slightest difference to the outcome of the game, and they both knew it. "The ball was inside," she insisted.

He grinned again. Close up, he could see thick lashes framing the gray blue of her eyes and accentuating the pale blush of natural pink on her cheeks. She didn't have a stand-out, flamboyant, knock-you-to-your-knees beauty, yet she had something unique, something of which she seemed totally unaware.

"The call stands," Jake said firmly, then shook his head when she stalked back to her position. All at once he became aware of his mother's hopeful eyes and winced. She was working on the after-game picnic, setting up a barbecue for hot dogs and hamburgers. Jake hoped everybody liked their 'dogs charred, because that was the only way Virgie could cook.

"Time's up!" he called a few minutes later.

Winners by five points, Cassie's Sea Avengers were ecstatic. He could see she'd taught her team to be gracious; in no time at all they were thumping their opponents' backs and congratulating them on a great game.

Virgie began banging on a large empty pan. "All right, you guys, time to eat."

Still full of energy, Cassie took over the barbecue grill and proved capable of producing a burger or hot dog in any preferred stage, from rare to charcoal. The cheerful bedlam quieted as the boys and their parents filled their stomachs.

Jake loaded his plate with potato salad and went to the grill. "Any hamburgers left?"

"How do want yours?" Cassie asked frostily.

Observing the large barbecue fork clenched in her fingers like a weapon, Jake decided it didn't matter. "Whatever you've got."

"Here." She slapped a massive patty on his bun. "It's a real man's size."

Virgie looked up and grinned. "Cassie's something else, isn't she, son?"

Jake sighed, wondering if a vacation spent with his matchmaking mother was really worth the trouble.

The next afternoon Cassie left the center early to meet her brothers, who were helping her move out to the cottage. She'd always wanted to live on an ocean bluff, hearing the sound of waves booming on the shore as she went to sleep each night. Now her dream was coming true, along with a few others.

When confronted, Virgie had reluctantly admitted to Cassie that her idea about Jake's becoming the donor father wasn't new. In fact, it had been hatched the moment Cassie had said she wanted to get pregnant. Offering the cottage to Cassie had been part of her scheme. After all, it would be nice to have her grandchild living next door... wouldn't it?

Thank heaven Virgie still wanted her to move in, despite the way her plan had been derailed.

At her apartment Cassie waved to the two men waiting by their respective pickup trucks, already loaded with furniture and packed boxes. As brothers went, Derrick and Steve weren't bad, though they tended to be bossy and act as if she didn't know anything a lot of the time. In her opinion that had less to do with being brothers than with being *male*.

"Ready?" Steve shouted, and she waved again.

"Follow me," Cassie called.

With each mile her excitement grew. There wasn't a lot of opportunity for change in a little community like Sandpiper Cove. She could get a job somewhere else, but she liked living in her hometown, where she knew practically everyone. And it was convenient to the coastal galleries that carried her paintings, which was important. Quite unexpectedly art had become a major portion of her income.

Virgie's house was located about eight miles out on the wooded peninsula north of town. There were numerous homes on the point, and Virgie's place overlooked a sweeping beach. Pines and undergrowth fringed the cliffs, partially concealing the structures above. The location was perfect for Cassie; she could paint and sketch to her heart's content, walk on the beach and maybe even get a large dog to run with her on the sand. Weren't children supposed to grow up with dogs and cats?

Virgie was waiting on her porch when they drove up, and Cassie pulled to one side to allow her brothers closer access to the cottage. They immediately untied the protective tarps and began unloading.

"Men of action," Virgie quipped, watching their silent, purposeful movements.

"Football game," Cassie returned. "They want to get done so they can go home, put their feet up and guzzle beer while they curse the opposing team and throw crushed cans at the TV."

"I love your close family ties."

"Yeah." She grinned. "Heartwarming, ain't it?"

"Shall we offer to help?"

"What, and offend their macho hides?" Cassie shook her head. "We'll just be fragile flowers of femininity while they sweat. In other words, I tell them where the stuff goes, and they break their backs lugging it there."

All at once a loud crash, followed by a deep bellow from the interior of the cottage, sent both Virgie and Cassie forward at a dead run.

"What's going on?" Cassie shouted.

Steve appeared at the door, brandishing a piece of wood. "This place is a wreck."

Derrick marched past, returning Cassie's antique steamer trunk to the truck. "You can't live here, Cazz. Half the boards are missing from the deck outside the back door. It's a straight drop down, more than thirty feet."

Right on cue, Jake walked around the corner of the building, minus his shirt and wearing a pair of faded, close-fitting jeans. A long two-by-four board was balanced across one shoulder, and a toolbox hung from the other hand.

"What's that about the deck?" he asked.

"It's a menace. My sister isn't living in a dump like this."

Cassie winced, Jake's face turned to stone and Virgie had the nerve to chuckle.

"Shut up, Derrick," Cassie snapped. "And take my trunk back inside."

"Like hell."

Getting close, she poked a sharp finger in his chest. "*Inside.*"

"Be sensible, Cazz," Steve argued. "You can't live here."

"That's my concern."

As much as Jake didn't want Cassie around as his mother's marriage bait, his pride was offended. Ignoring the opportunity to squash the deal, he stepped forward, furious. "This place isn't a dump."

"Like hell it isn't. Half the railing on the stairs just collapsed." Steve waved the piece of wood, and Cassie realized it came from the front staircase.

"Oh, no," she exclaimed, snatching the piece. "I told you to use the back stairs out of the kitchen."

"Excuse me for living."

She inspected the wood and saw it had just come loose from the fittings, not been splintered and broken. The stairs were half the charm of the cottage and she didn't want them ruined. Her fingers stroked the piece, then she looked up and took a deep breath.

"Please unload my things," she managed to say calmly. "Then leave. Get back to your TV before the game starts."

"We can't leave you here," Steve protested, but his words faded under Cassie's fierce glare.

"Now! I know the place needs some work, but that's part of my agreement with Virgie. I'm going to do a lot of the repairs myself for a reduced rent." She paused, then smiled with deadly intent. "Or shall I tell your wife the story of your twenty-first birthday party?"

He gulped, turning to his brother for support. Derrick looked in the other direction.

"*And* the pictures . . ." Cassie added for effect.

"You don't still have those?"

"In living color."

Steve was defeated, and Jake tried to keep from laughing. Her quiet exterior to the contrary, there was plenty of spice to Ms. Cavannaugh. She stood there defiantly, refusing to back down to the ill-mannered louts she called her brothers. The same way she'd defied him at the soccer game. Jake didn't want her in the cottage, but he admired her spirit; with male relatives like that, she might have turned out meek, mild and obedient.

To emphasize her point, Cassie grabbed a large box from the back of the pickup and lugged it into the house. Her younger brother let out a yelp and followed her with the air of an anxious puppy. "Lift with your legs," he could be heard scolding.

She stomped outside again and took another box. Despite the shapeless skirt and cotton sweater she wore, Jake began to detect a supple, pleasantly curved body to go with her firm derriere. On her third trip she reached up to pull a coat tree from the top of the stack, and the fabric pulled taut against those curves. He felt his jeans become tight, a definite danger in view of her two very protective siblings. *What will they do if they notice,* he wondered, *beat me into a senseless pulp or just push me off the cliff?*

"We'll get this stuff," Derrick protested, trying to take the coat tree from Cassie. If looks could kill, hers would have dropped him on the spot. "Aw, come on, Cazz."

"Don't call me that ridiculous name," she snapped, retaining her grip on the disputed piece of furniture and stomping into the cottage. She grumbled as she set the coat tree to one side. It would have been wiser to hire a mover instead of relying on her family.

From a rear window she saw Jake appear on the partially rebuilt deck, leaping agilely over the gaps between the boards. He began testing the strength of the wood on the far right, muscles moving beneath his tanned skin. Cassie's lips pursed in a silent whistle. He was gorgeous. Pure, grade-A, one hundred percent gorgeous. She was lucky he didn't visit his mother all that often.

You don't like him, remember?

Yeah, she remembered. Jake was a little too perfect for her taste, and his superior male attitude rivaled that of her two brothers. Still, Jake had dominated her dreams the night before with a sweet mix of passion and tenderness.

Dumb. Really dumb. She had no business fantasizing about him.

Taking the hem of her skirt, Cassie dusted the built-in chest fitted to the three sides of the bay window. The chest doubled as a bench, and when it was too cold and wet outside she could read or just sit and watch the changing pattern of the seasons.

The cottage was more than the name implied. The two-story structure had once sheltered a grounds keeper and his family. The main house where Virgie lived was all that remained of an earlier, quite magnificent mansion. Both homes were beautiful and solidly built, a testament to the determination and perseverance of the early Oregon settlers. The smaller house, which the locals called "the cottage," had been empty for a long time and was in a run-down condition, but that didn't detract from its appeal. What Cassie didn't know about repairs work, she'd learn.

"Cassie?"

She half turned and smiled. "It's all right, Virgie. I'm over my temper."

"You never stay angry for long."

"Don't I?" Cassie tossed her heavy braid over a shoulder, then walked to the kitchen and gazed out at the moving texture of the sea. The sun was setting, painting the water with streamers of pink and orange. Sometimes she didn't understand herself. There were voices inside of her, insistent voices of longing and need. Most of the time she didn't listen, but the crashing of ocean waves seemed to make them louder.

Soon the cottage would be filled with life again. The neglected wood would gleam with wax, the copper and brass come bright with polishing and the diamond squares of glass in the window would sparkle. Cassie would rock a baby at her breast, listening to the wildness of winter storms while the fireplace crackled with orange flames.

It was a compromise. A compromise with the longing of a romantic heart forced to accept the realities of today.

In and out of the cottage Steve and Derrick tramped, carrying the furniture and other belongings she'd collected over the years. Although they had planned to move her on two separate evenings, they went for the last load from her apartment and returned an hour later. With a rare sensitivity, they didn't pay any attention to Cassie as she stood in a melancholy dream at the window. The narrow rear staircase received some cursing, which barely registered in Cassie's consciousness.

Finally they stood awkwardly, shifting their feet and trying to get her attention. "Um . . . er . . . we're done," Steve said finally. "It's all here. Anything else?"

She almost laughed. "No, thanks. I think your game probably has started already."

"Oh, that's okay," Derrick assured.

"Thanks. Steve . . . let me know when Lisa goes into labor."

His face melted into boyish enthusiasm at the mention of his wife. "The doctor says the baby could come anytime. You'll be the first to know."

They left after giving her an awkward hug, which was the closest they ever came to apologizing for anything.

Virgie switched on the light, and the brightness of the bare bulb pierced Cassie's eyes. "It's getting late," she said unnecessarily. "Do you want some help?"

"No." Cassie smiled. "I've been looking forward to this for a long time. I used to dream about 'the cottage' when I was a kid, imagining how it would be to live here."

Virgie kissed her on the cheek. "Now you don't have to imagine. Welcome home, dear."

Home. What a wonderful word.

Outside, Jake was still working but he waved to Virgie as she crossed the yard, calling out something that made the older woman laugh. Cassie smiled slightly. No matter what other faults Jake had, he sincerely loved his mother. It was a definite point in his favor.

He'd strung some bright spotlights that illuminated the deck with a weird brilliance. Cassie glanced at the boxes needing to be unpacked, then back to the deck. A part of her wanted to believe Jake was trying to get her to notice him. If he was, it was working. Good Lord, the man had a sensual aura that turned her insides into warm honey.

At least he'd put on a shirt. They'd been having unusually warm days for fall, but evenings were still cold, and so far he hadn't bundled into anything more substantial. Determinedly averting her eyes, Cassie pushed up the sleeves of her sweater and got to work. With any luck she could get a lot of things arranged and put away before going to sleep. She'd taken the next day off, but there was a lot to do.

Fortunately she and Virgie had already cleaned the cottage from top to bottom. It needed paint, wax, stripping, sanding, polishing and a few hundred other things, but the place was clean. There was even shelf paper in the kitchen cupboards.

Jake pried another piece of rotten board loose from the frame, enjoying the hard physical labor. Crazy as it seemed, he was also enjoying the sight of Cassie through the uncurtained windows as she moved about the cottage, unpacking her belongings. She had a natural grace and elegance. He could give free rein to his libidinous thoughts now that her hulking brothers had departed.

A chuckle burst from his throat as he pictured their cowed expressions. There was hell to pay when Cassie lost her temper. He'd almost expected her to grab their collars and crack some heads together.

Strains of classical music crept out of the cottage. Low, seductive and enticing as hell. Cassie passed in front of the kitchen window again, sipping from a steaming cup. A thick braid hung to her waist, the color of old gold. She stretched, rubbed the back of her neck, then slid her tongue over her lips.

Damnation. Was she doing that deliberately? He'd wondered the same thing earlier when she'd stood at the window, staring at the sun setting over the waves. She'd waited until the last long ray stopped glittering, and the water was a steel shadow, reflecting back the lighter sky. She'd seemed distant, elusive, listening to something only she could hear.

Thinking about Cassie was far better than remembering his last security-consulting job. Jake sighed, trying to erase the images of destruction that still haunted him at odd moments. In his business there were always unpleasant memories. Too often he was called in *after* a tragedy...*after* criminals or terrorists had taken their toll on innocent lives—his last job was a case in point.

One. Two. Three. Jake pulled in deep, cleansing breaths, replacing the disturbing thoughts with Cassie. She had an intriguing innocence, though he couldn't, *wouldn't,* let it wrap around his heart. That would be too risky, no matter how sweet and fresh it felt.

But was she innocent? Maybe it was some subtle game she and his mother had planned between them. Forgetting to pay attention, he stepped forward. His leg slammed through an open gap in the framing. Jake cursed. An old nail had ripped through the denim and was lodged in his skin. Getting out was going to hurt a darn sight more than getting in, and that had hurt plenty.

"Are you all right?"

His head snapped around, and he glared. "Do I look all right?"

"No," Cassie said calmly, skirting the black openings similar to the one he'd fallen through. She knelt beside him. "What's the problem?"

"My knee is swelling, I've got a goddamn nail stuck in my skin, and blood is gushing off the end of my toe. Other than that, I'm fine."

The pain Cassie recognized. The anger, too. But she couldn't understand why he seemed so furious with her. Nobody made him work till all hours in the cold. Who did he think he was... Superman?

"Do you want me to call the fire department?"

His glare became blacker.

"I guess you *don't* want me to call them. I could get Steve and Derrick to come back.... They missed the first part of the game anyway."

No way in hell. Jake uttered a single profane word.

Cassie just shrugged. She'd heard far worse from her big brothers over the years. They had vocabularies most lumberjacks couldn't match.

"I guess I'll have to get you loose myself."

With caution she crossed to his toolbox, also retrieving the hammer. She then adjusted one of the spotlights so she could see better and crouched for a moment, thinking.

Cassie chose to work on the board behind Jake's leg, figuring it would be less painful than prying at the one holding the nail. Luckily the wood was just as rotten as the rest, and she was able to clear enough space for him to ease the limb free. He was right about the swelling knee but he'd exaggerated about the blood—it wasn't gushing, merely dripping.

"Come inside," she said softly.

"I don't need Florence Nightingale."

"No, you need your head examined. Stop being a stupid jackass and come in the house."

Her tone was cool, authoritative and said she didn't like him much. Jake pressed his mouth closed and hopped into the cottage. He noticed Cassie didn't offer to help, and she didn't say anything when he dripped blood on her kitchen floor, just tossed him a towel and pointed to an old ladderback chair. After a moment she disappeared. He heard the front door open and close, then open again. She reappeared with a businesslike first-aid kit and knelt beside his chair.

"From your car?" he ventured to ask.

"I work a lot with kids, and it pays to be prepared."

"Oh." Jake had the unpleasant feeling he'd been relegated to the status of a naughty child with a skinned knee.

Cassie's stomach turned as she cleansed the damage and did what she could to patch the torn flesh. "You should see a doctor," she said finally, wrapping gauze around the bandage. "And get a tetanus shot."

"I had one last month."

"Yeah, right."

"I'll make an appointment in the morning," he offered, hoping her expression would lighten and she might look at him with something other than frostbite in her eyes—maybe even smile. She really had a lovely smile.

For the first time in his life, Jake felt at a loss with a woman. *This* woman. A woman with two hulking family bodyguards and a pair of mysterious eyes. No wonder his mother had decided to go all out on her matchmaking efforts. But how could Virgie know he was a sucker for eyes like that? He hadn't even known himself.

Crash. Bang. Take a cold shower, Jake ordered silently.

Better yet, get out of the cottage before he did something foolish, like kiss the woman. He could probably wave his precious bachelorhood goodbye if he did...the Cavannaugh boys would round him up with a shotgun and haul them both to a preacher. At the thought, a delighted grin creased his mouth. Yup, they were the old-fashioned, protective sort. They'd probably wait until after the wedding before pounding him into a pulp.

As long as they wait until after the wedding night.

Jake jumped to his feet when he realized the dangerous direction his mind had taken him. The abrupt movement sent pain shooting up his leg, clear to his hip. It was a welcome distraction. He groaned.

"If you won't go to a doctor tonight, then take some aspirin and go to bed," Cassie advised. "I can repair the deck myself next weekend."

That did it. "The hell you will."

"I'm perfectly capable of using a hammer."

"I don't care what you're capable of, you're not going out on that deck until it's safe."

"I was just out there."

"You know what I mean."

"No, I'm just a dumb female, why don't you explain it to me?" Though her tone was sweet, her eyes were chilly.

Somehow or other Jake had worked himself into dangerous territory *again,* and it had nothing to do with the rotten flooring of the deck. Well, hell. He might as well be condemned as the old-fashioned macho jerk he pretended not to be. "It's a man's job."

Abruptly Cassie dropped back on her heels and... laughed. "You didn't do that right."

"Do what right?"

"The tough-male act. You need to throw out your chest more and thrust your hip forward." Standing, she did a parody of one of her brothers. "Then you use a tough, gravelly tone of voice and say, '*It's a man's job*.'" She grinned. "Just like that."

Jake sincerely doubted any man could move like Cassie and say anything in such a throaty, breathless voice. If he did it, he'd be arrested for making an indecent proposal. The words didn't matter, but the body language and tone said everything. And the really hellish part about hearing Cassie do it was that she didn't understand her effect at all. He could swear she wasn't intentionally enticing him or playing any games. For that matter, she didn't seem to have any interest in him as a man.

Yet he wanted her. Her variety of feminine subtlety and nuance was rapidly becoming his favorite flavor. Any minute now he'd burst out of his jeans and embarrass the living daylights out of both of them. Worst of all, she seemed oblivious to her effect on him. She wasn't embarrassed, and she certainly didn't appear to be looking—or deliberately *not* looking—at the blatant bulge at the top of his thighs.

"Do you—" His voice cracked and he tried again. "Do you ever listen when someone pulls that superior-male crap on you?"

"Nope."

He'd been afraid of that.

"I figure," she continued, "that anything a man can do, I can at least try."

Now was *not* the time to point out their anatomical differences, and the fact that there were some things, quite delectably, that she could and could not do just because she was a woman. Jake was getting closer and closer to a precipice he had no intention of plunging over. *No way.*

"I'd better go back to the house and take those aspirin." He yawned, pretending a weariness he didn't feel. "Mom must be wondering where I am."

"Probably," Cassie agreed. She didn't encourage him to stay, and Jake was foolishly annoyed that she didn't. What was the matter? Was she still angry about the soccer game?

Jake limped from the cottage and across the garden to the larger house. He paused for several minutes, letting the cold night air calm his arousal. The last thing he wanted was to have his mother see him looking like a randy teenager...even if he felt like one. It had been a long time since he experienced such uncontrolled lust. It was embarrassing, especially when the attraction didn't seem to be mutual.

Virgie was waiting for him in the living room, with a gleam in her face that had nothing to do with the hot chocolate she was drinking. The gleam turned to worry when she spied the torn, bloodstained denim on his left leg. "For goodness' sakes," Virgie exclaimed. "What happened to you?"

"I had an argument with a nail. I lost."

"I'll get some antiseptic."

"Don't bother. Miss Cavannaugh already cleaned me up."

Rampant curiosity lit her face. "Ah, yes, Cassie. She's so sweet. Very gentle and caring."

Jake wondered if he could fool his mother into believing his exhausted act. Probably not. "She seems very nice," he said, cautious. "Nice" was a good, noncommittal description. It certainly didn't suggest raging hormones.

"Mmm, yes. She has a natural maternal instinct. You saw how the kids on her team adore her."

Maternal instinct? Well, Jake supposed so. It was hardly the description he would have expected. Virgie normally pointed out how attractive, sexy and generously proportioned her candidates were. His mother had a healthy respect for sex appeal.

"I suppose most women are maternal," he muttered, at a loss to where the conversation was going.

"Oh, no, not all women. You'd be surprised. Cassie has a wonderful gift. But then she's good with people of all ages."

"I'm sure she is." *Where was this leading?* Jake didn't discount the value of maternal instincts and social skills, yet they were hardly subjects to tempt a confirmed bachelor.

"And she's very healthy. There aren't any inherited diseases in her family... good bone structure," Virgie mused as though to herself. "Long-lived...her parents were killed in an accident, but her grandparents on both sides lived into their nineties."

Jake rubbed his temples, a headache beginning to pound in his head. What did longevity and bone structure have to do with matchmaking? This was the most roundabout, unique matchmaking attack his mom had ever made.

"That's...er...nice," he managed to comment.

Virgie nodded. "Yes, and you're healthy, too. Good, strong genes."

"Okay, Mom." Jake leaned forward and captured her hands. "Enough pussyfooting around. Tell me what a wonderful wife Cassie would make, how happy we'd be, and how sexually satisfying a permanent relation is. Then I'll explain that marriage isn't for everyone, especially me."

"Oh, no!" Virgie pulled her hands free, frowned and took a sip of her hot chocolate. "That isn't what I was talking about."

"Sure."

"I promise, I really mean it. I've been thinking about what you said the last time... about not wanting to be tied down and everything. You're right."

"Mom—"

"No, it's true. Right now you can go anywhere, do anything you want, without any commitments holding you back." Her frown softened into a smile. "I understand wanting freedom. When I was young I had an itchy foot, too. Only women didn't wander the world when I was a girl, they got married and had babies."

Jake was astonished by her confession. She hadn't been the most conventional mother in the world, but she'd seemed happy. "I didn't realize."

"No, and I don't regret my choice. I only wish we could have had more children."

He knew the story, knew his mom had almost died with his birth, which was why Jake was an only child. "Lucky I was such a perfect kid," he teased. "I made up for all the rest."

"You certainly did. Except for not giving me a passel of grandchildren, you've been perfect."

Ah-hah. Jake felt more comfortable now that they were returning to familiar territory. He could handle his mother's matchmaking attempts. He wasn't sure he could handle soul-searching and honesty. Especially not now.

"Mother!" he said, a teasing, warning tone to the word.

"Er... Cassie is going to wring my neck for doing this." Virgie cocked her head to one side and shrugged. "Oh, well, she's a very forgiving person."

"About what?"

"Listen, son, Cassie wants to have a baby."

Right. He'd been right after all; sweet Cassie was in on the plan, and her supposed indifference was just an act. For some unaccountable reason Jake was disappointed. And angry. "So let her have one," he growled.

"She is! I don't mean she's pregnant right now, but she plans to get pregnant within the next month."

"Organized of her."

"She is and she'll be a fine mother. Of course, it doesn't always work the first time, and it seems such a waste for her to go to one of those places."

Those places? He wasn't going to ask what she meant; ignorance was safer. "Well, if she's made up her mind, I doubt we can change it." Jake rose hurriedly. His mother was getting craftier and more devious by the year. She'd have him hog-tied to Cassie Cavannaugh before he could run a mile, and with the injured state of his leg, running was out of the question.

"I have the perfect alternative."

Jake didn't even pause but limped straight for the door. "Good night, Mother."

"Son, it isn't what you think."

"Of course it isn't."

"Please... I just want you to donate the sperm for Cassie's baby."

Chapter Three

"What?" Jake felt as if he'd been body-punched and thrown across the carpet.

"Just donate the sperm. Cassie will sign a release of legal responsibility—she has to for the sperm bank anyway, and this way I can have a grandchild without you having to do much about it," Virgie explained in a rush, face hopeful.

"You want me to do *what?*"

Virgie sniffed. "Lower your voice, son, I'm old, not deaf." *Old* was a convenient expression she used, neither accurate to her state of mind nor her age of sixty-three. Jake wasn't buying it now or ever.

"Old? You aren't old, you're crazy!"

"Please be reasonable. I finally got the message—I know you don't want to get married again. Lord knows your ex-wife would convince anyone that marriage was hell."

The top of Jake's head felt as though it was going to come off. Could he have lost that much blood? Maybe he had. Maybe he'd actually fallen through the deck and broken every bone in his body. That was the explanation; he was in traction at the hospital and having a drug-induced nightmare. It was possible, and under the circumstances a nightmare was an attractive alternative.

"See? I do understand," Virgie continued in the same dogged tone. "You don't want to be tied down, but I want a grandchild. Cassie is a sweet, wonderful woman who would love your baby dearly. And I would get to play grandma to my heart's content. It's the best solution to all our problems."

"I don't have a problem!"

"Maybe not now, but in twenty years you'll look back and wonder what you did with your life," his mother retorted. "A child offers a sense of hope, a connection to the future. Cassie isn't selfish, she'd share that with you."

Slumping against the doorframe, Jake gathered both his hands into fists. He knew what a child offered . . . once he'd been thrilled with the idea. But not now. Not ever again. "I knew you were up to something, I just didn't realize your precious Cassie was in it up to her eyeballs, too."

He looked across at his mom, eyes narrowing. Or maybe this was all Cassie Cavannaugh's idea; she might have the mistaken impression the O'Connors had money. Sure, he was successful but he was far from rich.

Moving purposefully, Jake ignored the pain in his leg and marched back outside. He was going to have a few words with Ms. Cavannaugh and set her straight. He wasn't going to be treated like a prize stallion, valued for his reproductive potency.

"Son, stop."

He ignored his mother's cry and raised his hand to beat on Cassie's door. It was after midnight. The lights in the cottage were off but he didn't care. After a moment the front lamp switched on, and he heard a husky voice asking who was there.

"Jake O'Connor!"

She cracked open the door and looked out. "Yes? Doesn't Virgie have any aspirin?" Cassie yawned. She'd just been falling asleep when Jake began making a racket. Sheesh, he was a pain. He was rude to her, then he bled all over her kitchen and then he pounded on her door wanting over-the-counter medication.

"I don't want aspirin. I want to know what the hell you mean wanting me to get you pregnant!"

Her grogginess vanished. "Virginia!" she wailed, swinging the door wide open and glaring at the figure hovering behind Jake's wide shoulders. "How could you?"

"Calm down, there's no harm done," Virgie insisted.

Cassie emitted a combination scream and shriek and moan. "And I thought Phyllis Mulvey was bad at keeping secrets. You can't keep anything to yourself!"

To Jake this sounded like an admission of guilt, and his anger doubled. "You'll move out of the cottage tomorrow. I won't have a con artist attaching herself to my mother."

The blue in Cassie's eyes vanished, leaving only an icy gray rage equaling Jake's. "I am not a con artist, and this is all Virgie's idea—the cottage, moving here, asking you to donate the sperm. My idea was to get pregnant, pure and simple. I want a baby, there's nothing criminal about that."

Cassie was ready to scream—at herself, at Jake, at Virgie and her big mouth. She had felt so at ease with Jake when he was in her kitchen, and just minutes before, she had figured out why. Having decided to have a baby by artificial insemination, she'd temporarily put the possibility of romantic relationships out of her head. Even though she didn't really like Jake, a part of her responded to him. With her decision, she was free of worrying about what kind of feminine impression she would make and whether the guy was really interested.

Now this happened. So much for understanding the male sex and her reaction to them.

"It really was my idea," Virgie insisted, looking ready to weep. "Cassie didn't know anything until I sprang it on her at the center yesterday. She said no."

"I...I..." Jake tried to sustain his outrage, but it was hard. Cassie looked adorable in her anger—wearing a cotton T-nightshirt that barely skimmed the tops of her thighs. "It's a stupid idea."

"I agree one hundred percent," Cassie snapped. "I certainly don't want *your* genes in *my* baby. So thank you very much but I'll go to the sperm bank *like I planned in the first place!*"

"I wasn't offering. I'm not some kind of stud bull."

She wanted to laugh. Poor baby, he was insulted. He stood there with his chin jutted out, bloodstains on his leg and nursing an enormous, wounded male ego. Cassie threw an arm out theatrically, and looked him up and down.

"Welcome to the club," she mocked. "How do you think women have been treated for the last twelve thousand years? Like brood mares! Now, thanks to the miracle of modern science, men can be part of the breeding program, too."

Though Jake didn't know Cassie well enough to be certain, he thought she was acting out of character. Sure, she'd taken offense at his attitude about a woman coaching a boy's team, but that didn't mean she was a man-hater. And she'd teased him earlier, in a completely good-humored way about his old-fashioned point of view.

On the other hand, what did he know? He'd thought his ex-wife was the next thing to an angel...until she stabbed him in the back.

"Look," he began, trying to sound reasonable. "Why don't you ask one of the local yokels to do it, or don't you have a boyfriend who—"

"You're utterly despicable!" She was so angry now that the gray of her eyes had melted into a liquid silver. Any other time Jake would have imagined what color they'd turn with another kind of passion, but at the moment he was busy envisioning what destruction the two Cavannaugh brothers would wreak on his body for this last insult—and he didn't even know what the insult was.

Cassie discounted the confusion on Jake's face. How dare he imply she couldn't get a boyfriend. It was bad enough that he'd used that juvenile word, *boyfriend*. Lord knew, she was too mature to date boys.

"What did I say?" Jake asked, still trying to figure out his slip of the tongue.

"Nothing. Now, go away." She didn't seem to be in the mood for explanations. Her fingers curled around bunches of her nightshirt, pulling it even farther up her thighs without her realizing.

Jake realized. He was aware of every nuance of her long legs, slim hips and the hard-peaked swells above her waist. He almost groaned. Hormones—that's what he had—an excess of raging hormones, and Cassie was turning them all on at once. "I—"

"It's freezing," Virgie interrupted. "Cassie is going to get pneumonia if she doesn't have it already, which is a dreadful start for a baby. Can't we argue inside?"

"I'm fine, Virgie." But she wasn't; she had a healthy case of goose bumps from the cold October fog curling into the cottage.

Jake didn't even try to focus his eyes away. The worn cotton was molded to her breasts, leaving nothing of their form to the imagination. They were a lovely shape, ideal for cupping and holding and doing other heavenly things with his fingers and mouth.

"No, you're not fine." The elder woman spoke with all the maternal force she could muster. "Besides, Jake wants to apologize. Don't you?"

She poked him in the back, forcing his attention away from Cassie's more obvious charms. "Yeah, right."

All at once the door slammed in his face, and he winced. Cassie was furious, his mother was furious, his leg was in shreds and he was confused. Lovely beginning for a much-needed vacation. What else could go wrong?

"How could you do that?" Virgie moaned as she followed him back to the main house. "Now she'll go to that sperm bank, or else Phyllis will sneak her own son in."

"Phyllis who?" Jake asked, trying to be calm. Except for her matchmaking over the past several years, his mother was remarkably patient over his failings. Heaven knew he'd given her enough material to work with, but most of the time she showed a lot of restraint.

"Phyllis Mulvey. She and Lavinia and some of the others at the senior center want Cassie to consider their sons as donors."

Jake thought longingly of his quiet apartment. He sat on the sofa and contemplated driving back to Seattle, vacation or not. "Why aren't you shocked about this?" he asked. "My God, *I'm* shocked, and you're discussing it like a trip to the supermarket."

She snorted. "Give us old codgers some credit, son. Believe it or not, having gray hair doesn't mean you don't move with the times. If Cassie wants to have a baby, there isn't any reason she shouldn't. Besides, it's better than marrying that dimwit she was dating several years ago."

"What dimwit?"

"Local boy, I doubt you'd remember him. He works for the lumber company, and I think he's been conked in the head by a falling tree too many times. Good pecs but no brains at all, and sort of shy. He always reminded me of that country-music song about wanting a moron with talented hands."

He shouldn't ask. *Shouldn't*. "Does he?"

"Does he what?"

"Have talented hands."

"Not according to Cassie."

Jake's head began to ache in accompaniment with his leg and other parts of his body. "I can't believe she talked about sex with you. She seems rather...er...private." Except for her idea about getting pregnant with a sperm bank. Lord, had that really happened?

"What has sex got to do with it?"

"Mother," he began warningly, then caught the teasing glint in her eyes. "You know perfectly well what that song is about."

"You're right, and no, she didn't discuss it with me. I just . . . knew."

He presumed she was talking about some kind of feminine, motherly instinct, the sort of thing that he—as a man—wasn't supposed to understand. Hell. Maybe he didn't. In some ways a woman's body was a total mystery to him. So much of their response was hidden, out of sight, only felt by a man during the most intimate moments of their joining. Not to mention their ability to create and nourish a child.

A child.

Hellfire. Jake lurched to an upright position. He was not, repeat *not* intrigued by this whole idea. If becoming a husband didn't interest him, then fatherhood was even further down on his list of goals in life.

He hustled to his bedroom, forgetting his mother, forgetting the pain in his calf and muttering darkly. Insane, totally insane. Not just his mother, but himself for even listening to the cockeyed scheme.

Modern women—you could keep 'em. *Breeding program indeed,* Jake huffed to himself. Obviously Cassie Cavannaugh *was* an ardent feminist who didn't think she needed a man. Well, she needed a man to have a baby, but he sure wasn't going to be the unfortunate daddy.

Anger driving her, Cassie dragged the last box of dishes across the floor and began to unpack. She couldn't sleep, and ever since Jake and Virgie had disappeared across the garden she'd been working and freezing her rear end off. The heat in the cottage had inexplicably failed, leaving her cold and frustrated and downright unhappy.

I won't have a con artist attaching herself to my mother.

Insulting, nasty, distrustful man. Cassie felt free to thoroughly dislike him—before she'd felt a little guilty about it. After all, he was Virgie's son, and she was living on his mother's property. Too bad he was thoroughly unlikable. Oh . . . sure, he had a right to be upset about his mother's scheme. After all, it wasn't every day you're asked to get a total stranger pregnant in such an unorthodox fashion. But to react as he had? Yelling at her as if she were a criminal? Then implying she couldn't get a man of her own? Well, she had to admit she might have misunderstood that last part.

It didn't escape Cassie's attention that she ought to be angry with Virgie for plotting the whole thing. Yet at least Virgie had some excuse. She was alone in Sandpiper Cove, with infrequent visits to and from her son; no wonder she was anxious for a grandchild. Certainly she'd been plotting to get Jake married for some time—a daughter-in-law and grandchildren would help alleviate the loneliness. But despite his mother's most promising candidates, Jake had been remarkably elusive. According to Virgie, he considered love a vastly overrated myth.

Cassie pushed the last of the packing material into the boxes and shoved them out the side door. Crossing her arms in front of her, she leaned against the counter and surveyed the kitchen. *Wonderful*. The room just needed a little paint and caulking around the windows. All in all, the cottage wasn't in bad shape. A little loving attention was all that was necessary, provided Jake didn't succeed in running her off the property.

The fine line of her mouth tightened, a sign her brothers would have recognized instantly. True, Cassie tended to be quiet, and it took a lot to get her truly angry, but she had a stubborn streak that ran straight through her spine . . . and every cell in her body.

"I'm not leaving," Cassie growled. A wide yawn creased her mouth, and she wondered if she could finally get some sleep. Everything was put away, more or less in place and organized. Adrenaline had lent her speed.

She was just glancing at the clock when someone knocked on the door again. It was a quiet, almost tentative knock, so Cassie knew it couldn't be Jake.

Except it was.

"What do you want?" she said rudely.

Jake tried not to smile—he hadn't expected Cassie to look so cute and still so sexy. Her feet were encased in a pair of fuzzy "animal" slippers, her legs were still bare and her nightshirt was only partly covered by an enormous University of Oregon sweatshirt. He cleared his throat. "I . . . uh . . . noticed your light was on."

"So?"

"Is everything all right?"

"Sure, I'm usually awake at four in the morning."

He sighed. This wasn't going to be easy. "I just wanted to talk to you about . . . you know."

"About getting me pregnant? Don't tell me you've changed your mind?"

"No!" Jake exploded, then instantly regretted the outburst when she stiffened and scowled. He backed off a few inches, exercising the caution he'd use with an angry, spitting feline. "That's not what I mean. Not at all."

"Then why don't you say what you mean?"

"I've been thinking that I might have been wrong." Jake took a relieved breath. His words weren't quite an apology but they weren't another accusation. "About you," he added when Cassie didn't say anything.

"I'm . . . overwhelmed," she drawled, her voice dripping with artificial sweetness. "Imagine, you might have been wrong about me. *Might* have been. You're not sure but you're willing to admit the possibility."

Jake gulped and was glad she wasn't wearing enough clothes to conceal a weapon. He had the feeling she was mad enough to plug him. "I didn't mean—"

"I know, you didn't mean anything."

"Can I come in and discuss this?" he pleaded. "It's cold out here."

"It's cold in here, too," Cassie snapped. "The damned heat won't work. What did you do? Cut the gas lines?"

"How dare you question my integrity!"

"You questioned mine!"

Embarrassed, Jake loosened his collar. He'd made some ridiculous accusations and he had the feeling they were going to haunt him. "I'm sorry about that."

"You should be."

A sigh came out of his throat. He hadn't made much progress in making peace, and he very much wanted peace with Cassie Cavannaugh. He also wanted to slide his hands up her slender legs and discover the softness beneath the nightshirt. For hours Jake had lain in bed, imagining the silky sensation of her heat flowing against his fingers. He'd also cursed his lack of control.

Cassie felt the subtle shift of Jake's attention and fought to keep from squirming. His gaze drifted from her hips to the swell of her breasts beneath her sweatshirt. Her nipples hardened, and she couldn't blame it on the cold.

"Let's go inside," Jake said persuasively. He saw the softening in her eyes and willed her to agree.

"I . . . it's late."

"It's early. I'll try to fix the furnace."

For an instant Cassie almost relented, then panic tightened the muscles in her throat. *Damn him*. She didn't want to feel desire for him. Her decisions were made. If there was a man for her in the world, he wouldn't be someone like Jake O'Connor.

"Go away," she said.

"Please, Cassie, let's talk."

"I don't think you have talking in mind." She pushed the door closed.

Spinning, Cassie leaned against the wood and covered her face with her hands. How could he look at her like that— with such passion in his eyes—and so much distrust? And how could she respond, knowing he thought she was manipulative or even dishonest?

"I don't care," she announced defiantly. She also wasn't going to play his game. Filled with determination, she went to the kitchen and prepared a little "surprise" for Mr. Know-It-All O'Connor. With a sensation of glee she poured coffee into a thermos, snapped the lid on a plastic container, grabbed a cup from the shelf and opened the back door.

The crisp, ocean-scented wind blew tendrils of hair from her face as she cautiously stepped across the deck and set everything in the middle. The rotted boards looked treacherous, and the spots of Jake's dried blood were patent reminders of the hazard.

She hoped the framework supporting the structure was stronger than the surface planking. Cassie shivered, not from the wind but from the thought of having it collapse one day when she was out there with the baby. She couldn't take the risk. No matter how offended Virgie might be, the repairs would have to be inspected by an expert.

The sun was coming up, tinting the sky pink and trailing fingers of gold and silver, when Cassie finally climbed the back staircase and crawled into her rumpled bed. She thought about the future. The "baby" was as real to her as the ocean and the solid cottage that would shelter them both. Rolling to her side, she tucked the comforter tightly around her shoulders to ward off the chill of the room. Her mind sleepily imagined the moment when she would see her child for the first time.

Frustration almost kept her from going to sleep because her mind kept conjuring an infant with piercing green eyes. Just like Jake O'Connor's.

"You look terrible, son."

"Thanks," Jake mumbled, hunched over what his mother imagined was a cup of coffee. Since she didn't drink the stuff, what she called coffee came from an ancient jar of instant that had drawn moisture and consolidated into a hard mass. He rarely remembered to bring his own supply, which meant that on every visit he went through the ritual of watching her chip away at the contents of the jar until she had gouged out enough to color some hot water.

It was depressingly awful, but Jake had decided he deserved some punishment. A stranger might have had some excuse to fly off the handle by his mom's machinations...not Jake. He knew perfectly well what she was like— a heart of gold and the mind of a master spy. Cassie hadn't known what Virgie was planning, and the look of horror on her face should have been sufficient warning. So right now he was cursing his big mouth and drinking his mother's coffee in repentance rather than secretly dumping it down the sink.

"Breakfast?" Virgie held out a plate of charred bacon and something he presumed were eggs. Scrambled? No...he decided after a careful inspection, maybe they were just fried.

Did penitence require him to go that far?

"Er...um...I'm not very hungry."

"Suit yourself." She was still miffed over his behavior the previous night. So far, all her communications to him had been brief, pithy and lacking in sympathy.

Shrugging, she sat across the table and blithely began eating the food. She had the digestion of a garbage disposal; nothing ever upset her stomach. Virgie was gifted in many ways, and his parents' marriage had been extremely happy, but not because of her housewifely skills. Over the years she'd learned to wield a dust rag and vacuum cleaner reasonably well, but cooking eluded her.

She only offered food to Jake when she was displeased with him. Judging by the quantity she'd fixed that morning, he was going to be in hot water until he turned ninety.

Oh, well, he shrugged mentally. He might as well finish cooking his goose, since he was already plucked and thrown into the pot. "Mom..."

"What?"

"I don't understand. How can you want to be a grand-mother when you can't even make edible cookies?"

Her glance was frosty. "That's what bakeries are for."

"Oh. Well, yeah, sounds okay. I…uh…guess I'll get busy working."

He escaped as quickly as possible. Cassie couldn't possi-bly be as difficult as his mother, and he had to face her again at some point anyway.

But when he rounded the side of the cottage, he stopped short at the sight of something sitting smack, square in the center of the deck. He inched around the perimeter, as though a bomb was sitting there instead of an enormous thermos. *A thermos?* He circled again, not getting less than six feet from the object. Next to it was a plastic container and a stoneware mug. They seemed harmless enough.

Jake looked at the cottage, trying to see if Cassie was somewhere inside. He didn't see her. He didn't really ex-pect to see her.

A thermos. Thermoses usually contained good things; like milk, tea or even hot coffee. His mouth watered. He had the vague suspicion that Cassie, unlike his mother, made won-derful coffee. Edging forward, he nudged the steel bottle with his shoe. God, it was big—at least two quarts. Jake gingerly took the bottle and shook it. Full. Why had she done this?

He looked back at the cottage again, but everything seemed quiet. There was no classical music playing, and Cassie wasn't moving about the interior. Nothing.

Unscrewing the lid, he inhaled the heavenly scent of cof-fee—not just instant, but brewed. He sat down promptly and poured a full cup, his nose continuing to sniff in appre-ciation. It occurred to Jake that she might have put some-thing obnoxious—like hot pepper or salt—in the mixture, yet he couldn't resist taking a large swig from the steaming mug.

It was only coffee, but what coffee! A blend of different beans and, judging by the flavor, freshly ground; a man could get used to drinking stuff like that every morning.

The plastic container drew his attention next, and he popped the lid to find three cream-cheese-and-apricot Danish resting inside. They were exactly right with the coffee and filled the empty spot in his stomach nicely. He didn't let his questions about her motives impair his enjoyment. Time enough to wonder after he'd eaten the pastry.

The morning was much brighter with Cassie's addition, and Jake whistled off-key as he worked on the deck. He'd let the property get out of shape over the years. His mom had an inherent disregard for maintenance and anything mechanical. It wasn't that Virgie was dependent on other people; she just didn't seem to notice when sections of the roof blew away or when the car engine clugged and clanked.

"Cookies," Jake muttered to himself. Why had he asked about cookies? Virgie wouldn't be a typical grandmother... she was more the colorful Auntie Mame type.

It wasn't until midmorning that Jake saw Cassie appear, and she didn't even look in his direction. She was wearing another calico skirt and pullover sweater. She was yawning and moved automatically about the kitchen.

Just getting up? Jake felt guilty all over again. He'd been pounding and hacking at the deck—she couldn't have slept at all. He wiped his hands on a rag, went to the back door and knocked. Surely he was capable of a convincing apology.

The door swung open, and Cassie stared at him, eyes hostile. "What?"

Uh-oh. She didn't seem any more receptive than the night before. "I wanted to thank you for the coffee and Danish."

"Coffee?" She rubbed her eyes, then covered a yawn with her hand. "Oh, yeah, what about it?"

"Well... it was nice of you. Mom isn't much of a cook, and I really appreciate the gesture." Jake tried to sound utterly sincere.

Cassie was annoyed. Blast the man, he wasn't supposed to be grateful. He was supposed to be all prickly and suspicious that her little "gesture" was another ploy to get her pregnant or tie him into a commitment. She managed a sweet smile, even though her fingers had tightened on the door with the desire to slam it in his face.

"Your mother says I'm good in the kitchen, though I can't claim the Danish as my creation. You should come over some night and I'll fix you a nice home-cooked meal."

Jake tried not to laugh. Cassie wasn't much of an actress; there was a distinct edge of sarcastic resentment mixed with her tone and lurking in her eyes. This wasn't a lady on the make. She wasn't even interested. That, as much as anything, challenged and intrigued him—along with her incredible plan to have a baby on her own.

Good Lord, a sperm bank? She must know dozens of suitable fathers; why choose that way?

"Home cooking sounds great," he said casually. "How about tonight?"

Cassie's eyes widened and she almost choked. She hadn't been serious, and he certainly wasn't reacting the way he was supposed to react. Home cooking was supposed to make his native instincts rear their head and scream, "Take cover, your freedom's threatened." Hadn't he heard the old cliché about a man's stomach and the quickest way to his heart?

"I . . . well . . . tonight is—"

"Great!" Jake smiled and managed to keep his devilish amusement under control. He'd called her bluff, and it was going to be fun watching her squirm.

It had occurred to Jake that nobody could force him into marriage. This wasn't the 1800s, where shotgun weddings were the order of the day—no matter how many bozo brothers she might have. And there wasn't a reason in the world why he and Cassie couldn't have an interesting time together. She knew the score; his mother must have informed her of his aversion to sentimentality and the wedded state.

It also occurred to Jake that he was lucky Cassie couldn't guess his thoughts. She would have removed his head for such conceited thinking.

"I'll bring the wine," he murmured, watching the shifting color in her eyes. "White or red?"

Cassie's fingernails dug deep crescents into her palm. She didn't know any curses strong enough to fit what she felt Jake deserved. "White," she said through clenched teeth.

"Wonderful. This evening, then?"

"Can't wait," she grumbled, all too willing to wait forever for the pleasure of his company.

"You might try and sound a little more welcoming—my ego is beginning to feel bruised."

"I doubt if your ego could be bruised by an avalanche." Cassie's tone left Jake in no doubt that she considered him an arrogant ass with the sensitivity of a toad, and her abrupt honesty told him she was classing him with her brothers— which was something he wanted changed *immediately*.

He stepped forward, pulled her fingers free from their grip on the door and, before she could say yea or nay, planted his mouth over hers. Jake believed in the element of surprise, and this surprise had worked out to his extreme advantage. Her lips were open and pliant from shock, and they tasted better than he'd imagined possible.

Mmm. He gathered her closer, placing one hand over the gentle curve of her hip, with the other cupping the back of her neck. If he hadn't been holding her, he would have missed the faint tremor that shook her. *Little faker.* So, she wasn't interested. Her body was telling him different.

Jake slid his tongue over the edges of her teeth, tasting deeper. Wonderful. She'd added orange and cinnamon to her coffee, and the combination of flavors was a warm, lambent stroke to his senses. Quite reluctantly he stepped away a moment later and stared into her eyes. Right now they were the blue of the ocean, sparkling in the sun. A faint hiss of accelerated breathing issued through her mouth, drawing his attention.

"I'd better get back to work," he said, sounding hoarse and unlike himself. "I have to earn that dinner."

"Why did you do that?" Cassie whispered. Jake looked at her for another long moment, and she had the crazy feeling that finally—after all this time—she'd found a man who could look into her soul and accept all the storm and light that existed there.

"I don't know," Jake admitted with only partial honesty. The elemental male in him knew why he'd kissed her; Cassie's contradictory blend of sultry innocence astonished and aroused him beyond belief. He found it hard to believe a woman like that still existed in the world—a world where innocence was a joke, and where mystery and magic existed only in the minds of Hollywood film directors.

It was frightening because he had stopped believing in much of anything a long time ago and he hadn't even realized how much he'd lost. Where was the boy who had spent his childhood searching sea caves for pirate treasure and who was perfectly willing to accept the existence of wizards and invisible dragons? Gone, destroyed like his short-lived marriage.

"Tell me something," Jake murmured, reaching out and stroking the silky rope of braided hair hanging over her breast. "Do you still believe in impossibilities?"

Cassie could hear the confused yearning in his voice, the uncertainty beneath the confident man. She'd suffered after giving up some of her dreams and recognized the sorrow of someone who had sacrificed too many of them.

"Jake...what do you want?"

There wasn't an answer, because Jake didn't know. That was the hell of it; he just didn't know what he wanted. Like everything you lose a little at a time, he wasn't sure how to go back. It wasn't just a lousy marriage; it was working endlessly with security systems, hoping to save lives and property; it was shallow friendships and city life and everything else that was fast and furious and lacking solidity.

"I don't know that, either," Jake admitted slowly.

"You...you don't have to come to dinner tonight."

He shook his head. "You can't weasel out of your invitation so easily," he said, grinning a little to inject some humor into the tension.

Cassie could have pointed out that she hadn't exactly invited him, at least not with the serious intention of being accepted, but she didn't.

"All right." Unable to help herself, she lifted her hand and traced the sensual curve of his lips. She shivered as his eyes turned to green fire; reflected there were all the possibilities of being desired. Intensely. She understood some of what he wanted, and a hidden instinct was responding to the fire, savoring its heat.

His lips parted, and she stroked the damp inner curve before his tongue curled around her finger, sucking it deeper into his mouth. A work-hardened hand encircled her wrist. He acted as though the world were focused in the softness of her skin and the slender digit he was tasting.

He held her as she swayed, running his tongue into the softness between her fingers before nibbling ever so slightly. Her hips jerked toward him in a movement as instinctive as breathing. Never had she felt such incandescent heat, and he'd only touched her hand...still touched it, his eyes closed and attentive to the shivering leaps of her pulse.

"Jake?"

"Hush, Cassie."

He explored each finger; the pink curve of her nails, the sensitive tips—and each fraction of flesh was given the loving, lavish attention of his tongue.

Cassie needed to lean against something; there wasn't any strength left in her legs. She dizzily wondered why she'd never known the erotic possibilities in a person's hand. Jake did, and seemed to know exactly what he was doing to her.

"I don't think...I have to...Jake!" she said urgently.

There was nothing smug in his expression as he eased her into a nearby chair—ironically the same one she'd planted him in the night before when he'd hurt his leg. In fact, he looked just as shaken as she felt, which wasn't what she expected of someone with his legendary reputation . . . a reputation Sandpiper Cove had learned of in great detail, thanks to his doting mother.

"It's okay," Jake breathed. God, he wished they were in bed at this moment. Did Cassie have any idea of how he wanted to feel her around him, so tight and hot he could die from the pleasure of being inside her?

No, she couldn't know, and she couldn't know the abject panic his need made him feel. He wanted her and yet he wanted to distance himself from the way she opened up a vulnerable, empty part of his soul he'd forgotten existed.

Hell and damnation. This wasn't the way his vacation was supposed to go. He was supposed to rest and get his perspective back. He had a life away from Sandpiper Cove. He didn't need anyone, especially someone as sweet and gentle as Cassie.

"Jake?" Her fingers framed his face, and he felt the lingering dampness from his own mouth. "What's wrong? You look . . . angry."

His smile was forced. "Not angry. But I'll tell you one thing, Cassie Cavannaugh—you're a dangerous lady, very dangerous. I don't know what to do about you."

"I'm just me."

His smile became ironic. "I know. That's what worries me."

Chapter Four

After Jake smashed his fingers for the third time with the hammer, he realized his assessment of Cassie was too mild; she wasn't just dangerous, she was an outrageous menace to the health of his mind and body.

Didn't he already have a jagged hole in his leg to prove the point?

The problem was lack of willpower. Show him a woman who could make a great cup of coffee, and he was hooked; give her eyes like Cassie's, and he was a goner.

So why wasn't he running?

You can't leave—you promised you'd stay the month. Jake grinned wryly—he should have gone to Hawaii. Surely his mother's manipulative plans negated his promise. Especially after Virgie had faithfully sworn that she wouldn't do any more matchmaking.

Oh, hell. She wasn't matchmaking this time; she was plotting his fatherhood. Maybe he should just say yes. That would give her heart failure...which would be a fitting punishment to the shock she'd given him. *I just want you to donate the sperm for Cassie's baby.* Imagine, asking him to father a child by a woman he'd hardly met, a small-town lady who divided her time between senior citizens and children.

The hammer slipped and hit his forefinger this time. "Damn it all to hell!" he said out loud. He stood and tossed the hammer in the general direction of the toolbox.

If he ever said yes to that ridiculous scheme—which he wouldn't—he'd want to get Cassie pregnant in the much more enjoyable old-fashioned way. And he had no doubt that it would be enjoyable. He'd seen enough to know that only her exterior was demure; inside she was fiery enough to melt the polar ice caps.

Jake flexed his sore fingers, then limped off the deck. He had an appointment to see a doctor about his leg. Hadn't he promised Cassie? Then he was going to visit the drugstore; getting her pregnant wasn't in the books, but making love to her was a definite possibility. *Definite.* He wanted to be prepared, and the hell with how arrogant that sounded. There was no way he was going to get her pregnant accidentally.

That's what worries me.

What had he meant by that? Was it some kind of obscure warning? Cassie frowned and continued chopping the onions and celery. Her eyes were smarting from the onions, but she ignored the irritation and finished the job. She wished she could ignore Jake as easily; her hand still tingled from the concentrated caresses he'd lavished hours earlier. Lord, the man could turn the most unlikely places into an erogenous zone.

The deck still wasn't finished, which was the least of her concerns. The telephone was installed, the furnace repaired, the packing boxes removed to the dump and her old apartment was cleaned and scrubbed, but she was still edgy. She blamed it on Jake.

Cassie didn't mind cooking for the man; she loved to cook. No, it was more the *idea* of his coming for dinner, especially when she'd expected him to react like a nervous bachelor around a prowling female. Just then the telephone trilled softly. She answered, hoping it was Jake calling to say he wasn't coming after all. "Hello."

"How's the new house?"

"Lisa!" Cassie grinned, delighted. She tucked the receiver under her chin and started to slice the mushrooms. "How are you feeling?"

"Enormous. I'm going to give birth to a full-grown football player."

Cassie clucked sympathetically. Her sister-in-law was one of her favorite people. "Steve seemed fine last night, but we didn't talk much. Is he still having jitters about being there when the baby is born?"

"Let me put it this way," Lisa said dryly. "I had some indigestion this morning, and *he* was the one who threw up."

"Serves him right."

"What did they do?" Lisa's tone was resigned.

"Oh, nothing much . . . they told me I couldn't move into the cottage."

Her sister-in-law laughed. "I'm sorry I missed that. No wonder Steve looked so meek when he got home. What did you do?"

"I threatened to tell you about that twenty-first birthday party of his. You know, the one where he got drunk and took his jock strap—"

"I know," Lisa interrupted hastily. "You get more mileage out of that party. One of these days I'll have to tell him I know all about it."

Cassie thumped her knife down on the counter. "Lisa Bailey Cavannaugh, don't you dare. I need something to keep him in line."

"You're going to need more than some embarrassing pictures when he and Derrick find out about your pregnancy plans."

Uh-oh. Cassie sank down on one of the kitchen chairs. She'd forgotten that news of her plan would be flying around Sandpiper Cove at lightning speed—which meant that Steve and Derrick would hear sooner or later. Cassie would prefer later. *Much* later.

"Does . . . uh . . . when do you think they'll find out?"

"Probably tonight. If you're lucky, they won't know until tomorrow. I've been trying to intercept the calls, but Steve is getting suspicious."

Cassie's groaning response was unintelligible.

"Hey, if you wanted to keep it a secret, why did you tell Phyllis Mulvey?"

"I didn't. Virgie did."

"Just the same, you may as well have advertised in the newspaper."

"I know." Cassie sighed. She'd hoped her brothers wouldn't find out until *after* she was pregnant. Nothing they said was going to change her mind, but they were going to make her life miserable in the meantime. "Thanks for the warning."

"Uh . . . Cazz . . . for what it's worth, I understand. And I'm all for it."

"Thanks." She smiled as she replaced the receiver. Lisa was a sweetheart, and most of the time Steve didn't deserve her.

Cassie finished slicing the vegetables and threw them into the pot to brown with butter and curry powder. Almost everything was ready; she only needed to wait for Jake to arrive before putting the dish together.

Turning off the heat beneath the pans, she walked upstairs to change and comb her hair. She did everything without thinking, too busy listening for one of her brother's trucks to arrive in the driveway. They would yell so loud everyone in Oregon would hear the explosion.

Distracted, she almost jumped out of her skin when the doorbell rang. It couldn't be Derrick or Steve, since they would shout the house down. She hurried down the staircase and peered cautiously through the leaded-glass window before opening the door.

"Good evening." Jake gave her a slow, sexy smile full of promise. In one hand he held a bottle of expensive wine, and from behind his back he pulled a bunch of flowers. "For my lovely hostess." There was a faint twinkle in his green eyes.

Cassie felt like beating him over the head with the flowers. "Thanks," she said, sounding less than appreciative. "Come into the kitchen. Dinner will be ready in a few moments."

"Smells good."

She walked ahead of him, hips swaying in unconscious provocation. Jake sighed. Six hours hadn't cooled him down a single degree, while Cassie was back to being downright prickly. He supposed he shouldn't have wangled the invitation, but there were lots of things he shouldn't have done over the years.

The cottage had undergone a transformation in the past twenty-four hours. Jake was astonished both by the change and the elegant simplicity she'd wrought in the old structure.

"Very nice," he pronounced.

"What?"

"No clutter, I like it...or is all that stuff still packed away?"

Cassie turned up the heat, then stirred chicken into the curry-vegetable mixture. "Everything is unpacked. I don't have a lot of knickknacks."

Thank God for that, Jake silently affirmed, but it wasn't what he'd expected. "I thought everyone in small towns collected junk. Isn't it sort of a tribal law?"

"Snob," Cassie retorted without rancor. "I was raised by my maternal grandmother, and she was a champion collector of 'junk.' I had to dust everything once a week and it would take me hours. I vowed my kids would never be subjected to such torture."

Jake frowned. He knew she wasn't reminding him of her plan for having a child, yet it bothered him just the same. "So you don't have any knickknacks."

She shrugged. "A few. In the living room I have a seventeenth-century English bed warmer and a French spinning wheel. And there—" Cassie pointed to where shiny copper pans and utensils graced the wall "—I have an utterly useless collection of decorative cookware."

"Those hardly qualify. You have expensive taste, Miss Cavannaugh. How do you afford them?"

"Not by working at the senior center."

"I guessed that."

Turning, she directed her attention to the food, knowing he was expecting an explanation he wasn't going to get. She still felt a lingering resentment about his accusations the previous night. Con artist? Well, he had the artist part right.

"Why don't you open the wine?" she suggested, pulling the corkscrew from a drawer. Turning back to her cooking, she ignored his glinting smile.

The wine gurgled as Jake poured generous portions into the goblets. For good measure he lit the candles waiting on the table, unable to stop fantasizing about making love to Cassie by candlelight. Hell...why stop with candlelight? There was always firelight, moonlight and reliable old electric light. He came up and looked over her shoulder, though there was plenty of room at her side. "What's for dinner?"

"Chicken curry. I hope you like spicy food."

He allowed his hand to graze the inward sweep of her waist. "I *love* spicy."

"Back off, O'Connor," she warned.

"But you look so lovely." The corners of his mouth twitched. "That beautiful dress and frilly apron—quite the little homemaker. And heart-shaped earrings...they're so very romantic."

"I am romantic." Cassie stirred the mixture before adding the remaining ingredients. Heaven help her, they'd be lucky she didn't burn their meal if he kept breathing in her ear. "Which means I'm not your type."

"That isn't strictly true." Jake touched the length of hair she'd clipped away from her face. It hung in a shimmering curtain down her back. His fingers tangled in the silk strands, scented and cool to the touch. Provocative. "I smell hyacinths...right?"

A shiver began at the point where he touched her, then arrowed straight to the base of her stomach. Drat the man, didn't he know anything? Her outfit was supposed to scare him off, not turn him into a seductive monster.

"Yes, and I'm still not your type," she insisted, filling their plates. "I believe in romance and marriage and happily-ever-after." Cassie dropped her foot back and crunched the instep of his foot. He winced. "Did I mention I'm also clumsy?"

"You did that deliberately."

Her smile was seraphic. "Of course. Hungry?" She thrust a plate into his hands, which was a safer occupation than touching her.

Jake hadn't paid attention to the food, but when he looked at the mixture his mouth watered. The exotic dish Cassie had chosen was both fragrant and artfully arranged; saffron-flavored rice formed a ring on the plate, and a creamy curry sauce filled the center with chunks of pineapple and chicken. She had the right condiments, as well, including a jar of homemade chutney.

All at once he laughed. Cassie was using all the ploys of an old-fashioned girl—not to attract him but to scare him away. It had to be one of the most unique brush-offs he'd ever received in his life.

"What's so funny?"

"Nothing." Jake spread coconut, raisins and peanuts over his plate and dipped a fork into the concoction; it was delicious and spicy-hot enough to wilt a lesser man. Luckily he'd spent a lot of his career working in places where highly spiced food wasn't the exception but the rule.

"Do you cook like this every night?" he asked after he'd filled his plate a second time.

Cassie sighed and rubbed her face. She'd been silly to think Jake was going to retreat—he'd seen through her act from the very beginning. And in a way it was interesting being the object of such a persistent seduction.

"Just every other night."

"Terrific, I'll be over day after tomorrow."

"I didn't invite you."

"You don't really think that matters, do you?"

"To you? No."

He chuckled. "Cassie, my darling, you're beginning to understand me. We're going to be great friends."

"Friends? I thought you had something warmer in mind."

"I certainly do. I'm glad you don't object."

Her mouth opened and closed in quick succession. "I do object," she said stoutly. "I'm going to have a baby—I can't have an affair with you."

"As much as it pains me to point this out, you aren't pregnant yet." Jake swallowed the last bite of his curry, then looked at the pot where a considerable portion still remained. He wanted more, but his stomach was filled to bursting. "Can we have the leftovers for lunch tomorrow?"

"No." A car revved on the road and Cassie gave a startled jump.

Jake noted the distraction in Cassie's face, then decided—regretfully—that he wasn't the cause. "Something wrong?"

"Wrong? What could be wrong?"

"Darned if I know."

Cassie gulped the last of her wine. She was trying to think of ways to convince Steve and Derrick that she was making the right decision. If possible, she wanted their understanding and support; having a child alone was going to be tough enough without fighting them every step of the way.

Jake leaned forward and filled her glass again. "Drink up," he murmured, waving the bottle at her.

"Huh? Oh..." Her fingers flexed around the goblet and she absently swirled the contents.

"Cassie?" he said, but she didn't respond. He leaned back in his chair and addressed the ceiling. "I'm eating dinner by candlelight with a beautiful woman, and she won't even talk to me. Some gratitude after I risked life and limb to repair her deck."

A reluctant smile curved her mouth. Jake had a lot of charm when he turned it on, and he wasn't bad in the humor department, either. "I was just thinking," she began.

"Think on your own time."

Another car went by, and Cassie flicked the tip of her tongue across dry lips. "It might be a good idea if you left."

He frowned. "Why would I want to do that?"

"Because I'm expecting my brothers any minute, and it won't be a social call."

"Ah..." Jake said, his body refusing to budge. "You planned an extra surprise for tonight. I get confronted by the hulking bodyguards, determined to know my intentions toward their little sister."

"No," she retorted. "I'm going to get screamed at, yelled at, bullied and harassed about having a baby. You haven't seen fireworks until you've seen Steve and Derrick get their sense of propriety damaged."

"Then I'm definitely staying... you need the moral support."

"You don't approve any more than they do."

"At least I acknowledge your right to do what you want."

"Thanks, but you're not my brother."

Jake leaned across the table and uncurled her tight fingers from around the goblet. "Thank God for that." He dropped a moist kiss in the center of her palm. "Because I don't feel brotherly toward you."

Sensation snaked up her arm and through her body. "I can't," she whispered, feeling helpless and aroused and unsure of everything, even her fondest dreams.

"Can't what?" He stroked the fluttering pulse in her wrist.

"I can't sleep with you."

"Why, Cassie?" Jake slid his fingers up the sensitive skin of her arm. He wanted to distract her, make her forget her brothers. He wanted her to forget everything but the two of them. "Because of the baby? Can't you postpone those plans for a while?"

"No!" Cassie snatched her arm away. "I can't."

"I—"

All at once there was the squealing sound of brakes being applied too quickly and truck doors slamming.

"Cassie!" A fist started banging on the front door. "You damned well better let us in there!"

She groaned. "Jake, leave by the back door."

"Uh-uh, I'm staying for the show."

Pausing at the kitchen door, Cassie glanced back as he followed her. "Show? It's going to be a rip-roaring fight, nothing else."

"That's what I mean." He looked at her, an odd smile playing on his lips. "You don't know, do you?"

"Know what?"

"How—"

"I'm going to kick it in!" Derrick shouted, continuing to pound the solid wood.

"Just a minute."

"You don't have a minute."

Her eyes rolled. "Jake, I really advise you to leave. They're mad enough without adding fuel to the fire." She walked to the front door, opening it so quickly that Derrick pitched forward, landing in an untidy heap at the bottom of the spiral staircase. Steve landed on top of him. She nudged them with a disdainful toe. "Get up. You look ridiculous down there."

Jake couldn't help himself; he burst out laughing. Didn't those idiots know they weren't a match for Cassie? But of course they didn't. She might dread their interference, even hate the battle, but once she lost her temper they were goners.

The two Cavannaugh brothers glared at Jake. "What are you doing here?" Steve asked with heavy tones of suspicion.

"Trying to seduce your sister."

Cassie gasped. Steve and Derrick leapt to their feet. "O'Connor! You're gonna be sorry you ever lived," one of them yelled.

As they started forward, Cassie landed a hand on each of their aggrieved masculine chests. "Not in my house you don't."

"Stay out of this, Cazz."

Her fingers yanked on their shirts. Though she hadn't a fraction of their strength, they didn't break free. "I said *no!* It's none of your business."

Derrick's mouth dropped open. "None of our business? Did you hear what he said?"

"Yes. And whether I go to bed with the man or not is my business. You have nothing to say about the matter."

"Like hell we don't."

"Let them go, Cassie darling, I'm ready for them." Jake meant it. He was itching for action, but whether he meant to defend Cassie or himself or exorcise some personal devils he couldn't have said.

The "Cassie darling" startled them all, but not for long. Steve and Derrick digested the endearment as a personal affront, and Cassie decided Jake had a death wish, one she wasn't going to accommodate. She didn't need his protection, though she realized he had neatly deflected their attention from her proposed pregnancy. Temporarily at least.

"Stop it, all of you." She retained a firm grip on their shirts. "If you're going to fight, then do it on the beach where you can't damage anything but each other."

"I said to let them go, Cassie."

She turned her head and looked at him. "Jake, I think you ought to leave."

"We haven't had dessert . . . yet." The inflection of his voice left no doubt about what he wanted for dessert.

"Have some ice cream with your mother."

He crossed his arms over his chest and leaned against the wall. "I don't think so."

"Cazz, you can't be serious about this guy," Derrick barked. "You know his reputation."

"I'm *not* serious about him. I hardly know the man," she cried, utterly frustrated. "We just had some dinner. And you're a fine one to talk about a reputation. What is it they call you in the locker room . . . 'In and Out' Cavannaugh? Or is that just your bedroom style?"

Jake snickered, and Derrick's face turned a brilliant red. Obviously he hadn't expected his little sister to understand the sexual overtones of that particular nickname.

"And you—" Cassie shook the hand holding Steve by the collar, "—you were worse than Derrick before you married Lisa, so don't you say another hypocritical word. I'm a grown woman and I'll do what *I* want to do, not what you think I should do."

Something in her words caught their attention, and they looked down at her. "Speaking of which . . . what the devil is this plan to have a baby?" Steve growled.

Satisfied they no longer planned to attack Jake, Cassie released her grip, stepped back and raised her chin. "Exactly that. I want a family and I'm going to do something about it."

"You have a family," he said sharply. "You have all of us and you're going to have a new nephew or niece any day. You can baby-sit all you like."

"It isn't the same."

"Tough. Wait for a husband, then have your family."

"Right," Cassie said almost bitterly. "Wait forever and then end up with nothing."

"You could have gotten married. It isn't our fault you didn't."

"I've never been in love. And if I want children, I have to start now. I'm not getting any younger."

Derrick snorted at his brother. "It's that idiotic biological-clock garbage. Cazz, just wait. You know what grandmother always said about finding the right man."

No one but Jake noticed Cassie's shivering, so he quietly shrugged off his jacket and set it across her shoulders. He wanted to jump into the argument and yell at the two men opposing her, but this was a battle she had to face alone. In a few weeks he would be gone, and if she was serious about this baby, she'd be fighting a lot in the next year.

Cassie caught the edges of the coat, appreciating the warmth and subtle support Jake had unexpectedly offered. "I remember. Grandmother always used to say that everyone had a special someone they were meant to be with," she said. "Well, I've waited. And *waited*. Where the hell is he?"

"I don't know, but you won't find him if you're carrying another man's baby!" Derrick snapped.

"Maybe I don't care anymore."

"Maybe you've just lost your mind."

"Maybe you should all go to hell."

"Please, Cazz...don't do something you'll regret," Steve pleaded.

Regret? There were a lot of things Cassie regretted, but having a baby wouldn't be one of them. God, she was tired of their smug interference. For the first time she wondered if staying in Sandpiper Cove was a mistake. She could live in the city or go to work for one of those big international relief agencies. With her background in social work, there were a lot of options.

"I'm having a baby," she said very clearly and distinctly. "It's not open for debate." Cassie turned and walked up the staircase. She wanted to be left alone. She didn't want to be continually reminded about lost dreams and might-have-beens.

The torment on Cassie's face made Jake feel crazy. She was like a rare flower—exquisite, a contradiction of fragility and strength. That she could be related to such insensitive lug-heads went beyond comprehension.

"I think you've done enough damage," he growled when they moved to follow.

"This isn't your concern," Steve said.

"I don't give a damn whose concern it is—you've upset her enough for one day."

"Cazz is planning something very stupid. We won't let her do it."

"You can't stop her."

"My God! You're planning to be the father!"

"I've been asked to consider it," Jake admitted, not mentioning it was his mother's idea. He was more than willing to take some of the heat onto his shoulders. He felt his family was partially to blame for Cassie's current problems. After all, if his mother didn't have such a big mouth, Cassie's plan would still be a secret.

"You get my sister pregnant, and I'll... I'll..." Derrick spluttered furiously, apparently unable to invent a punishment dire enough for the supposed crime.

"You can't do anything, so why don't you just leave?"

Cassie lay on the bed and stared at the ceiling, dry-eyed. The sounds of a muffled argument ended with a slamming door and the angry revving of a truck engine. She shouldn't have left the three men together, but she'd taken all she could stand and Jake had contributed with his own nonsense about trying to seduce her.

"You okay?"

Her eyes closed. "Perfect, can't you tell?"

Jake sat next to her on the bed and leaned against the brass headboard. He didn't understand the comfort he felt with Cassie—in spite of the curious storm she kindled in his heart and body. "They left," he said unnecessarily.

"They'll be back."

"Not tonight, I hope."

"No, not tonight." Her voice was flat, lacking its usual lilting quality.

He sighed, wishing things were different, wishing it was Cassie that he'd met all those years ago, before his faith in marriage and fidelity was destroyed. Yet all those years before, he would have never recognized the treasure—he'd only wanted the gilding.

"It isn't true," she whispered, and Jake took her hand, lacing their fingers together. The softness of her skin was a startling contrast to the callused hardness of his own.

"What isn't true?"

"That I don't care about finding someone." Cassie swallowed, wishing she could swallow the ache in her throat. "I still want that. I want to find the special someone I grew up believing in. I remember my parents...they were so happy—like God had created them to be together."

"You've never been in love?"

"A couple of times I thought so. But I always knew, deep inside, that it wasn't real."

Lifting his other arm, Jake pulled her close. He could feel the shivers she was trying to control, just like before, during the confrontation with her brothers. "Why the baby?"

"Do you ever feel...like you're just on the sidelines? Just watching while life passes by without you?"

Jake didn't know what to say. He moved at such a furious pace he never had time to wonder if life was passing by him. Yet...in a way he could understand. She meant the elemental thread of life and not the modern values of money and success. "You feel that way?"

"More and more, though my mind tells me I shouldn't. I work at the senior center, trying to make a difference. Two nights a week I coach the Sea Avengers, and I volunteer time at the hospital. My friends joke and laugh and tell me how lucky I am not to have the commitments of marriage and children. I can paint and be creative and do anything I want with my time. They talk like it's some great choice I made.

I'm the only one who thinks it isn't great and that it isn't a choice."

Cassie turned and curled around the hard planes and angle of his body, molding to him in a uniquely feminine way. Jake held her, knowing she didn't mean to arouse him, just that she needed the comfort of his warmth and presence. Anyone would have sufficed. Yet her innocence seduced him, just as her honesty plucked at his heart and renewed the fear he'd felt before, when she'd looked too closely into his soul.

Her fingers played with the buttons on his shirt, and he held his breath, certain she would feel the rushed pumping of his heart. Cassie didn't need his passion, not tonight.

"They don't realize how lonely it is to go home each night and not have anyone there...no one to share the responsibilities, the joys and pains, no one to lie beside and hold. Do you know...I've never slept through the night with a man?"

Jake shifted and hoped she wouldn't realize what a powerful effect her words had on him. "I'm not sure you should be saying this to me," he warned, struggling to keep his voice from cracking like an clumsy teenager's. "Tomorrow...you might be sorry."

She considered the possibility. "I've never said those things before, not out loud," Cassie breathed. "But it's so easy to talk to you, and I don't know why."

A lot of reasons presented themselves to Jake; he wasn't sure he liked any of them. "Perhaps you're telling me the things your brothers wouldn't listen to. I'm sort of a substitute—you need to talk to someone, and I'm the only one who's handy."

He was handy, all right, too handy. Beneath her ear she could hear the heavy thump of his pulse, meeting hers beat for beat, and Cassie could easily imagine they were two lovers lying together. It was a lovely fantasy—a lovely trap. He wasn't her lover and he didn't understand, but then no one ever had. She had always been considered an "odd" child. Too well she remembered her grandparents' mur-

muring together, the long sideways glances at the little girl who wouldn't cry, even on the day of her parents' funeral. Only in the secrecy of her room, late at night, had the tears come.

"They won't ever listen," she said so quietly Jake almost didn't hear. He wished he hadn't. The emptiness of the words spoke of new hurts and old loneliness.

"I'm listening," Jake surprised himself by saying. "Maybe I was wrong, and it's easier talking to someone you don't have to face every day. You know, a stranger."

A faint laugh slipped from Cassie's tight throat. "Stranger or not, you're the kind of man I've always...well...felt uncomfortable around." She almost said "the kind I've never liked," but changed her mind. She was beginning to like Jake too much.

"Oh? What kind of man is that?" Jake felt her shrug, so slightly he wasn't even sure she'd moved. "Cassie?"

"I don't know—it's hard to put into words. Confident. Very masculine. Very self-aware. Someone who's got everything and doesn't need anybody."

Unintentionally Cassie's sketch of Jake's character sent pain ripping through him. Is that how he appeared? Self-contained and self-absorbed? There were names to describe that kind of man... like *arrogant*. And without much effort he could come up with something even more suitably descriptive. Hell, he was so arrogant he even had condoms in his wallet. Fresh ones.

"I'm sorry," he whispered, wanting to say much more and yet unable to conjure the words.

"You've nothing to be sorry about, and I haven't felt that way since you hurt your leg. Angry at times, but not uncomfortable."

"Good.... But not about the angry part."

"Why not? You deliberately annoyed me more than once."

He laughed. "True, but you were so certain you'd scare me off with that little homemaker routine, I couldn't resist.

Now, just out of curiosity, why am I out of the running as a potential husband...not that I'm volunteering, you understand."

"No, of course not," Cassie agreed, humor edging her tone. "You're out of the running because confirmed bachelors are too hard to housebreak."

"Be serious." When she didn't respond, he shook her a little. "Why?"

"Maybe...maybe I don't want a broken heart." This time she was serious, and it made Jake think.

"I wouldn't..." He paused, thinking hard. He'd been ready to promise he'd never break her heart, yet how could he make such a promise? He wouldn't do it deliberately, yet it could happen. "The same could happen to me," he said finally.

"No, I don't think it could."

"Why not? Everything is two-way." When she remained silent, Jake cupped her chin, turning her face to look at him. "Why, Cassie?"

"Virgie says you don't believe in love...that you call it a myth. Is that true?"

He couldn't lie. "Yes...at least for me."

The sad sweetness of her smile washed over him. "Then that's why."

Chapter Five

"Don't mind me," Cassie said, pulling away slightly. "It's none of my business."

Jake shrugged. "It doesn't matter. But you're right, I don't put any faith in love. It's too easily lost. But that's what you want, what your friends have. There's nothing wrong with it." *Until someone's heart gets broken.*

Cassie shook her head. "You don't understand. I don't want an ordinary kind of love, but something so powerful it burns into your soul and without it you're incomplete. And when two people find one another, like separate halves of a whole, anything can happen."

"Then why aren't you willing to wait?"

Feeling the tension in Cassie's body, Jake cursed his unruly tongue. He didn't have any right questioning her choice; he was just a disinterested observer.

Disinterested?

The blood rushing to the top of his thighs contradicted his blaring self-protective instincts. But even more than the arousal he couldn't deny, he also felt a kinship with Cassie. They both knew too much about lost hopes.

"Forget I said that," he whispered, his fingers sliding through her silky hair. "You don't have to explain."

She relaxed slowly. "Maybe this *is* just the biological clock, but I keep thinking about holding a baby, feeling it move inside of me. It hurts, because I don't have any of the things that are most important to me."

"So you're settling for a part."

"Yes." Cassie rubbed her cheek on his chest. "I don't want to compromise, but I will if I have to." Her tone was edged with determination, and once again Jake sensed the strength beneath her fragile exterior.

"I don't know...having a child alone, that's rough." She quivered again, and Jake gathered her closer, tucking his jacket tightly around her shoulders. "Sorry, I shouldn't have said that, either."

"It's okay, you can't say anything I haven't told myself a thousand times. I know it will be hard, yet I'm more scared not to do it."

He nodded. "What about the cost? The senior center can't pay much, and kids are expensive."

"I have a second income . . . from my painting," she confessed. "The sales are mostly in small, coastal art galleries, but I'm doing well."

A memory teased Jake, and then his eyelids shot open. "Wait a minute. That watercolor in Mother's living room— the seascape, did you do that?"

"Yes."

"Holy smokes," he breathed. "It's fantastic. I'm crazy about that piece." He meant every word. The painting was filled with glowing light and movement, drawing the eye again and again. No wonder Cassie was "doing well."

"Thanks." She sounded neither particularly pleased nor indifferent to his praise, and he realized painting was just something she did for pleasure—no great passion or long-held dream, unlike her dreams of love. Abruptly he felt anger expanding in his chest. Why couldn't Cassie dream of possibles? Why did she make him ache for her unrealized hopes?

Cassie sighed softly. She could get addicted to having Jake hold her in his arms, but it didn't take any great intuition to know he wasn't the right man and they weren't the right arms. No matter how kind he was now, she sensed he didn't approve of her decision to have a baby any more than her hardheaded brothers.

"I shouldn't have left you with Steve and Derrick," she said quietly. "This isn't your battle."

"I probably shouldn't have provoked them. They were mad enough as it was."

Remembering the expression on her brothers' faces, Cassie began laughing.

What are you doing here?

Trying to seduce your sister.

"It was worth it. You should have seen the way they terrorized my dates when I was in high school. They made Attila the Hun look tame."

"I'll bet." Jake eased his arm from her warmth and got off the bed, trying to suppress his anger. It was irrational and pointless. He shouldn't be upset, shouldn't care what she did with her life.

As she watched his motions, Cassie sensed the suppressed energy he was trying to conceal. "What's wrong?"

"Nothing."

"I'm sorry I sounded so maudlin about everything." She bit her lip. What did you say to a man after you've told him your most intimate secrets? He was a stranger and yet not a stranger. "I'm not unhappy. Most of the time I'm fine. It's just that the past few days have been so hectic, and I'm kind of stressed. You must think I'm neurotic."

"Don't worry, I don't think anything of the kind. I . . . I should go. You need to get some rest."

Without even looking at her or waiting for a response, Jake strode to the bedroom door; moments later the front door closed behind him. Cassie chewed her bottom lip. Curious man. For all his seductive, distrustful ways, he was tender and caring. There was a great hunger in him that had nothing to do with sex and everything to do with unanswered questions.

She scrambled upright, feeling tense. Her hands closed around Jake's jacket and her lips quirked in a melancholy smile.

"Chivalry isn't dead," she told the silent room.

Combing through the tangled length of her hair, Cassie braided it loosely, then climbed out of her skirt and sweater, and into jeans and a heavy sweatshirt. She hooked Jake's jacket on the coat tree at the bottom of the stairs as she slipped out the side door. She needed to walk on the beach. Maybe the waves would help soothe her nerves.

Jake tucked his hands into the pockets of his jeans, feeling like a jerk. He'd tried to comfort Cassie, and when it got too much for him, he'd disappeared like smoke in a blizzard. He felt even worse when he saw her leave the cottage.

The air was cold, and the wind blew with persistent force, streaking clouds across the sky and blurring the moon. Cassie was bent against the wind, fighting it to go down the rough path that led to the beach. Jake frowned. It really wasn't safe to go down at night.

"She ought to have more sense," he muttered to himself, shifting his feet uneasily.

His instincts, both professional and personal, screamed at him to drag Cassie back inside her precious cottage. Too many things could happen. She could be blown off the path. A maniac could be on the beach, waiting for someone to come along. Somebody could have a gun or a knife, and then her precious dreams would be worthless because she'd be dead.

"God," he groaned, deliberately hitting his head against the solid wall of the house to knock some sense into his brain. He'd spent an entire career solving security problems—trying to thwart thieves and terrorists, crazies and coldly calculating criminals. The chances of someone like that being on the beach were practically zero.

She could still fall.

You're overreacting.

There's no guarantee the beach is safe. There could be danger, no matter how improbable it might be.

His alter ego kept arguing with him as he skirted the cottage and followed the same path Cassie had taken. Jake knew if he examined his motives closely he'd find his actions had nothing to do with ensuring her safety.

When he finished scrambling down the narrow path, he saw Cassie in the distance. The breakers were white in the scattered moonlight, and the foaming water curled into her path as she walked.

"Damn-fool woman," Jake growled, plowing ahead. No wonder the Cavannaugh brothers tried to keep her on a short leash; she didn't use the sense God gave her. "Cassie!" With the wind whipping the sound away, she didn't hear him, and he broke into a dogtrot.

"Cassie!" As he grabbed her arm, she screamed and stumbled. Jake yanked her upright. "It's me," he shouted when she pushed against him.

"What are you doing?"

He didn't answer right away, since he was too busy staring at her bare feet and the jeans rolled to her knees. "Are you crazy? It's freezing and you're wading in the water!"

"I happen to like the water," she quipped through chattering teeth.

His fists clenched for a second, then he dragged her above the reach of the breakers. What he wanted was to shake some common sense into her beautiful head. "Haven't you ever heard of sneaker waves? You could be knocked over and dragged out before you knew what was happening."

"Hasn't happened yet."

"I think you have a death wish."

"I think you're blowing things out of proportion. I walk on the beach all the time—I know what I'm doing. Besides, you're the one who doesn't have a coat."

"Argghh!" Jake kicked through a pile of sand and seaweed. "It's the middle of the night."

"I know, I needed to think."

"Well, think about this!" He yanked her into his arms and kissed her, deep and hard, with all the pent-up anger and frustration he couldn't restrain. And longing. Her lips were cold and salty with sea spray, but inside her mouth was an essential, sweet warmth he wanted to devour.

Cassie, what's happening?

As though in answer she raised her arms and held him just as tightly, yielding to his hard contours. She had a natural, enthusiastic talent for kissing, and at least one part of Jake's body felt as if it were going to explode from sheer pleasure.

Idiot. Stop holding her, stop touching her. You can't be what she wants.

He ignored his conscience—just as he'd ignored his alter ego—and sank with her to the sand. It was cold but less exposed to the wind than standing, and he covered Cassie's body with his weight. She moaned and shifted, adjusting to him. Her restless fingers explored his shoulders and the muscles in his back.

"Jake..."

"I'm sorry I yelled," he muttered the apology. He moved, stroking the curve of her waist, seeking and finding the hem of her sweatshirt. The soft fabric slid upward, exposing the lacy bra confining her breasts. Carefully he unfastened the hooks and brushed it aside.

"Doesn't matter."

But it mattered to Jake. "I'm not...not like...your brothers," he said disjointedly. "I'm really not."

"Oh, I know...they'd *never* touch me there."

"What, here?" He caught her nipple between his thumb and forefinger, squeezing with exquisite care.

Cassie arched beneath him, her breath ragged. She didn't feel the cold of the wind or the damp chill of the sand beneath her hips. All she cared about was the line of fire Jake was drawing—from the skilled exploration of her breasts to the heavy, denim-covered bulge he was pressing between her legs.

"Here?" he repeated, tracing each mound with teasing strokes.

"Yeah..." she gasped finally, "there."

He pushed the sweatshirt higher, shielding her sensitive flesh from the wind as best he could. The wintry air—or desire—crinkled the velvet of her nipples even tighter, and he gloried in their responsive texture, testing their hardness with the edge of his teeth.

"You taste good," Jake breathed. His tongue licked her sensitive skin, tasting and teasing until Cassie thought she would go insane. At the last moment, when she thought the sensual ache would splinter her completely, he drew one throbbing tip into the heat of his mouth, plucking the other with a gentle, controlled stroke.

Cassie squirmed. Combing her fingers through Jake's dark hair, she held him, unwilling to let go for even a moment as the sweetness of his caress twisted and burst into a thousand flames. "More," she whispered.

He wanted to hold her in more ways than he'd ever thought possible. Only the knowledge that they were on an October beach, in the middle of the night, kept him from stripping the jeans from her legs and plunging into the silken haven of her body.

Reluctantly he let the velvet bud slide from between his lips and felt her twist in instant protest.

"No..." Cassie shivered, her voice breaking with the cold and abandonment of Jake's mouth. "Please...no..."

"*Think*," he said, fighting both their desires.

"I don't want to think."

Her knees rose, and he instinctively settled against the nest she made for him. He groaned with longing. She was so enticing. Her gentle innocence was like chasing laughter and sun-warmed days on sandy beaches.

She still believes in dreams.

For a last, lingering moment Jake let his knuckles graze across Cassie's nipples, then he caught her face between his hands, determined to put an end to something he should never have started. "This isn't what you really want. Tonight was awful. Your brothers trying to bully you. Me playing my stupid games. Do you really want to make love with a stranger?"

"I . . . you're not a stranger."

"No? Think again. I'm the guy arrogant enough to buy fresh condoms in case I needed them for tonight. Want to see?" Jake reached back and fished his wallet from his pocket. "Check it out, not just one, but four of the damned things."

He flipped the connecting packages so they landed on her bare breast, and Cassie flinched. "Put them away."

"You mean I won't be using them? Not even one?"

"I mean you're acting like a jerk. I'm cold," she said thinly. "Get off of me. I want to go back to the cottage."

Jake knew he'd won, but he'd also lost spectacularly. For all his harsh words and deliberate antagonism, his body still wanted Cassie. He was pressed against her so hard he was in danger of splitting his jeans. The moonlight had painted her skin silver, and shimmering wisps of hair curled about her face. The darkly crowned centers of her breasts were taut, shadowed and mysterious in the luminous light.

"I mean it," she repeated when he didn't move. "Get off me, or you're going to lose something vital."

"You can't get your knee around that far," he said, unperturbed. The safest, if not wisest, course at the moment was to stay put and not move until she calmed down. He couldn't blame her. He'd deliberately aroused her with every ounce of skill he possessed, leaving them both in an aching state of need.

Cassie squirmed, trying to dislodge him without success. He was right; she couldn't get her knee into the critical position. "Move!"

"No. Are you a virgin?"

She stopped wiggling and stared, astonished. "What?"

"Are you a virgin?" Jake asked, belatedly realizing he had no business asking and certainly no right to expect an answer. It was just the first, idiotic question that had popped into his head.

"That's a horrid thing to ask!"

"I wasn't trying to insult you," he said mildly, softly removing the packets of condoms and easing the sweatshirt over her breasts. He'd enjoyed the feel of her moving against him, but now was hardly the time to renew a seduction he'd already squashed. Besides, even though his back was angled to block the wind, it was still cold—too cold to be lying around with bare skin.

"That isn't the first time you've implied I couldn't get a man," she snapped.

"What? I've never . . . What gave you that idea?"

"Last night," Cassie huffed, forgetting she'd decided he hadn't meant anything of the sort. "You asked why I didn't—*couldn't*—get a boyfriend to get me pregnant. Like I was incapable of attracting a man."

"I didn't say you couldn't attract a man. Hell, you're doing a great job with me. Part of me is begging to make a baby with you. That *is* what it's all about, you know," Jake murmured almost to himself. "The biological imperative. Our instincts tell us to perpetuate the species, and to make sure men do it they give women bodies like warm satin and eyes that hold a thousand mysteries."

"Then any woman—"

"No, not any woman." His thumb stroked wisps of hair from her forehead, followed by his lips. "We've outwitted those instincts with contraception. The result? Uncomplicated sex between consenting adults. Freedom. Then you

come along, and make a man want to be naked inside of
you, without any barriers."

"But..."

He hushed the trailing word, flicking her lips with the tip
of his tongue. "Naked with you Cassie, knowing he's
pumping life into your body and wanting it to take hold."

The breath caught in her throat. She was filled with a kind
of wonder—and despair. Jake spoke of desire and instinct
but not of love. He didn't believe in love. He didn't believe
in forever-afters. And it shouldn't matter. They were just
two people whose lives lay in opposite directions.

"Jake, what do you... I don't know what you want."

He shifted his hips, pushing his arousal against her. "No?
I thought my problem was obvious. But you're so innocent."

Innocent? Cassie lifted her head and tried to read his eyes.
He said the word like a talisman. Swallowing, she tried to
ease the hurt and disappointment crowding her throat. She
hadn't thought Jake held that particular double standard.

"Not hardly," she said tightly. "Mind, with brothers like
Steve and Derrick I could easily have ended up as the
world's oldest virgin. I may not sleep around much, but I
know where all the parts go. If I was innocent, I wouldn't be
lying here with you in a position that could only be viewed
as... erotic."

"Babe, innocent girls lie on beaches all the time with men.
That's how they lose their innocence."

"Is it... is it that important to you?" she asked, biting her
lip with fierce concentration.

"What?"

"Virginity and innocence. Wake up, it's the twentieth
century. A maidenhead is no longer a commodity... or at
least it shouldn't be."

"That's not what I meant," Jake said quickly, realizing
she'd misunderstood. It was obvious someone had hurt her
badly, crushing the romantic ideal a girl holds for her first
lover. His fingers flexed into a fist as he felt a primitive de-

sire to punish the man who'd taken her virginity, then callously stamped on her heart.

"Right," she snapped.

He framed her face with his hands, looking deeply into her eyes, shadowed in the faint light. "Right. Oh, Cassie, you have a wonderful innocence, clean and fresh. I think it's the way you look at life."

"I look at it the same way everyone does."

"No, not everyone." Running his hand along the gentle curve of her body, Jake felt her tremble with more than the cold. He'd never known a woman so responsive, so generous with her passion. She loved being touched; he'd discovered that already. And she loved touching; her fingers had traveled over him with unabashed pleasure.

"Dreams," she said flatly.

"Yes, dreams. You say you're willing to compromise, and perhaps you are, but you'll still cling to the dream. You have a vision of perfect love and rose-covered cottages. Happy endings. Life isn't like that. It's real and hard and just plain dirty. You take what you can get and forget the rest."

His harsh summation should have made Cassie angry, but instead she was appalled. He'd lost; he'd battled his demons and lost. "Jake, don't—"

"No!" The single word of denial was filled with torment. It was so tempting to be with her, to just forget and be free. He could give her his baby, and she wouldn't demand anything in return. Jake buried his face against Cassie's neck, breathing deeply. The scent of her skin was sweet with perfume, the taste tangy from salt spray. It made him feel desperate. "I'm not offering you anything."

"I didn't ask."

"No, you didn't have to. Your eyes ask. You're driving me crazy."

"I am not."

"Are too."

A muffled shriek came from her throat. He'd lifted himself above her, and Cassie pushed at him. The unexpected pressure tumbled him to the sand. She scrambled to her knees and glared when he laughed.

"This whole thing was your mother's idea. You would never have looked at me otherwise."

"I'm looking now."

"Who cares."

"Ten minutes ago—"

"Ten minutes ago I was out of my mind." As hard as she tried, Cassie couldn't keep a note of rueful humor from her voice.

"Best way to be." Jake rested on one elbow. "Just so it's perfectly clear, I'll spell things out. I'm willing to sleep with you, Cassie, but I'm not willing to get you pregnant. And you won't get promises of commitment. I'm free and I intend to stay that way."

Her expression turned from wry to furious. Once again he'd succeeded in making her angry, but it was a hollow victory.

"I told you before, I'm not asking. You aren't the end-all, be-all object of a woman's dreams, Jake O'Connor. In fact, you're spouting the most arrogant load of nonsense I've ever heard."

He stayed silent, fighting the temptation to soothe the rough honesty he'd thrown at her.

"Nothing to say?" Cassie reached under the sweatshirt and fastened her bra, then yanked the shirt down again. She hadn't noticed the cold before, but now it was creeping into her bones. Mist had gathered, shrouding the beach and muffling the ceaseless roar of the breakers. "I'm not a fabulously beautiful woman, yet I've had my share of men try to seduce me. You do it with more skill than some, but you've got a fatal problem in the seduction department."

She paused, waiting, expecting him to ask. He remained quiet.

"A woman knows when a man's eyes dismiss her. She knows when he doesn't consider her beautiful or exciting enough to satisfy him. Believe it or not, some women find that a major turnoff."

Jake couldn't stop himself. "I never dismissed you."

"You did. When we met at the senior center you made me feel like a drowned waif."

"I didn't . . . that's ridiculous."

"Of course you'd say that. What is it, Jake? Are you lowering your standards with me because there's no one else available?"

Some vicious swear words slipped out of Jake's throat. "Some jerk really ran a number on you, Cassie, but don't lay the blame on me. All right, so when we first met I didn't start drooling. But it didn't take me long to discover you're the most desirable woman I've ever met, *including* my ex-wife."

It was Cassie's turn to be silent.

"Well?" he demanded. "It isn't like you went out of your way to attract me. How was I supposed to know? You were hiding behind that damned napkin, red in the face and layered under a shapeless sweater and skirt. Excuse me for not yanking you onto the table and stripping off your clothes."

"That isn't what I wanted," she whispered.

Jake groaned. Why couldn't he keep his mouth shut and hands to himself? The answer was painfully obvious. He'd told the truth: she was the most seductive lady he'd ever known. Not just her body—however delectable—but her soul. The way her eyes expressed every emotion and still kept secrets. Cassie was the fire of a desert sun and the silver satin of moonlight. She was storm and calm, softness and the hard-edged strength of steel. She was a mixture of contradictions that would terrify most men. Jake was no exception.

"I'm sorry," he breathed. He wanted to apologize for all the men who had hurt her in the past—men like he'd always been. Blind, seeing only the obvious, never looking below the surface. "I didn't dismiss you," he said, feeling helpless, repeating the denial that was partly true, partly a lie.

Cassie struggled to her feet, ignoring Jake's extended hand. She didn't want to hear anything more. And she knew she'd better get good at ignoring Jake O'Connor, because she wasn't going to be driven from the cottage. After lying on the chill sand, her muscles didn't want to operate, but she brushed the lingering grains from her jeans and marched toward the cliff path.

"Cassie, please."

"Leave me alone." A moment later she disappeared into the fog.

Chapter Six

Jake leaned his head against the new four-by-four post he'd installed at the corner of the deck. His vacation wasn't turning out to be very restful. And it was Cassie's fault. Now that he knew the supple warmth of her body, it was driving him crazy.

Sex. Pure and simple.

Oh, yeah? his conscience snarled at him. Then why did he hate the fact that Cassie was avoiding him? She hadn't even been subtle about it. If she caught one sight of him, she snapped around and marched in the opposite direction. Since she was a "forever" kind of woman, he should have been thrilled.

"Damnation," he muttered. Cassie despised him, and his mother was walking around with a perpetual scowl. Neither woman was cutting him any slack.

Jake lifted his hammer and examined it. He knew that hammer intimately; it had landed innumerable times on his thumb and fingers. Each time he let his mind wander and think of how Cassie had looked that night on the beach—

mysterious, provocative, her breasts stroked by silver moonlight—he lost control.

Sighing, he let the hammer drop and glanced at the cottage. His mouth twisted into a wry smile. The expert at sophisticated, short-lived affairs was fantasizing over Cassie Cavannaugh like a teenager.

Good going, O'Connor.

Cassie frowned and threaded the curtains she'd purchased onto the rods, then hung them from their brackets. The hammering from the deck had temporarily ceased. Cautiously she peeked out of a window overlooking the deck and saw Jake sitting on the outside edge. Okay, fine. She was proud of herself. Two days ago she would have hoped to see him, clinging to the edge and bellowing for help as he dangled over the precipice. It was major progress.

Cassie frowned again. Maybe it wasn't progress. Today she couldn't help noticing how the morning light accentuated his tanned shoulders. He looked just like one of those television commercials displaying sexy construction workers with rumpled hair and sculpted muscles. "Doesn't he ever wear a shirt?" she grumbled.

She'd successfully dodged Jake for over three days. He hammered on the deck; she went to the senior center. He worked on his mother's yard cutting back the undergrowth; she coached her soccer team or stayed in the house. It wasn't hard; she just pretended he didn't exist.

Liar.

"Shut up," she ordered herself. Okay, so she wasn't pretending he didn't exist. It was hard to ignore someone like Jake... he had a personality like a hurricane.

Cassie stalked back and forth across the floor like a caged cat. She didn't have any excuse to leave the house. It was her day off at the center, and the Sea Avengers weren't practicing that night. She needed to relax. *Had* to relax. The problem was having to wait now that she'd made her decision about the baby. It was hard to wait when she'd waited all her life.

Rubbing her arms, Cassie climbed the stairs and stepped across the platform at the top into the small room she'd chosen for a nursery. It wasn't finished. The walls still needed painting, and the hardwood floor had to be sanded and waxed. But, next to the window, a dainty bassinet sat waiting for an occupant. It was the only thing for the baby she'd allowed herself to buy.

"In good time," she murmured, sinking to her knees and touching the bassinet. The day would come when the nursery was filled with colorful mobiles and toys, all the things a child would need. A yawn Cassie couldn't quite control stretched her mouth. She was so tired. Too many hours had been spent sleepless, thinking about Jake.

Sunlight streaming through the diamond windowpanes had warmed the air in the room, though the light was becoming diffuse from the cirrus clouds collecting in the sky. Cassie rested her head against the window seat, allowing herself a brief fantasy. An expectant mommy and daddy were joyfully decorating a nursery. At night they cuddled under warm quilts, making love and anticipating the future. They loved each other more than anything else in the world.

She yawned again and tucked her arm under her cheek. As fantasies went, this one wasn't bad. Her eyelids drooped. It was warm and cozy in the sunlight.

Perfect.

Several hours later Cassie woke to the sound of heavy wind striking the cottage. She stretched and looked out, acknowledging the swift change in the weather with the acceptance of a native Oregonian. Sun in the morning, storm in the afternoon. There was nothing surprising about it.

She heard the high-pitched whine of an electric saw and grimaced. Jake was still out there, working away and keeping her trapped in the cottage. Drat the man. Didn't he have any friends to keep him busy? How long did it take to fix one little deck?

Don't you *have any friends?* her conscience taunted. *Anything to keep* you *busy?*

Suddenly she was not only furious with Jake, but with herself also. She'd let his presence control her life for the past several days. Well, not any longer. Without stopping to get a jacket, Cassie stormed down the stairs and out the side door. Keeping her eyes straight forward, she headed for the path to the beach.

"Cassie?"

She ignored him.

"Cassie!" Jake's hand closed around her upper arm and pulled her to a stop. From the corner of her eye she could see he'd put on a shirt and suede leather jacket. In a more reasonable state of mind she might have breathed a sigh of relief—a bare-chested Jake would have been harder to resist.

"I'm going for a walk. Alone," she announced.

"Talk to me," he insisted.

"We have nothing to discuss."

On a fundamental level Jake knew Cassie was right. But he couldn't stop himself. "It won't just go away." He knew he'd caught her attention when she turned and looked at him, her eyes mirroring the stormy, slate-blue color of the ocean.

"There's no 'it' and nothing to 'go away,'" she snapped.

Jake resisted the urge to shake some sense into her. "Damn it, we nearly made love the other night."

"Thanks for pointing that out. I'd completely forgotten," Cassie returned sarcastically. "Of course, you were strong and noble and resisted temptation."

He winced. "I wasn't being noble. God, Cassie, I wanted—still want—to be with you. It's just that... well...I'm..."

"Just forget it."

With a lithe twist of her body, she evaded his grasp. The wind caught her at the head of the path, molding the soft cotton of her skirt and sweater to her feminine curves. Jake groaned. He doubted Cassie had any idea of her effect on him.

All at once he frowned. He was a fool to keep thinking about her...desiring her. She wanted a *baby,* for pete's sake. He didn't have time in his life for a baby, much less a woman like Cassie. It was ridiculous.

"Idiot," he cursed under his breath, stomping back to the cottage. He glared at the deck. He should have been finished with the repairs three days ago. The thing was jinxed.

"Aren't you going to follow her?"

Jake spun around. He glared at his mother as though she'd deliberately crept up on him. "What do you mean by that?" he demanded.

"What do you think?"

Damn. He should have known she'd notice his preoccupation with Cassie's activities. Her matchmaking instincts were always on target. "I think you're hoping for something that won't come true," he said bluntly. "I'm not getting Cassie pregnant and I'm not going to marry her."

Her eyebrows raised. "I didn't ask you to marry her, just get her pregnant."

"Well, I'm not going to do either. Period. I'm just worried about her safety. It's an occupational hazard. That's what I do, remember? I'm a security consultant."

"Of course, son." A small, self-satisfied smile curved Virgie's lips.

Jake tried to control the embarrassed heat creeping above his collar. Turning away, he put his hands on the railing and gazed seaward. The storm was breaking, tossing waves onto the shore with breathtaking force. A familiar tensing of his stomach began when he couldn't see Cassie. Every night she walked on the beach. For hours. She followed the tide like a magnet to steel. And he followed Cassie. Watching her...wanting her. He felt like a fool, grasping at beams of moonlight. But he also felt responsible for driving her to those endless walks.

"Son?"

He turned his head.

"She's all right." Virgie motioned to the seemingly deserted stretch of sand below the bluff. As if denying her words, a brilliant fork of lightning lit the sky, streaking down until it met the sea.

Jake rubbed his forehead. "Sure."

"I *am* sure," Virgie said slowly. "Cassie understands the ocean . . . she isn't in any danger. It didn't kill her before. It won't now."

Though distracted by the thought of Cassie alone on the storm-swept beach, Jake was struck by the curious comment. *It didn't kill her before.* . . . He opened his mouth to request an explanation, but his words were drowned in a crash of thunder. Rain sheeted across the landscape, threatening to drench them both.

"I'm going to get Cassie," he shouted. "You'd better go inside."

Jake followed the trail back to where Cassie had descended. He saw her below, kneeling on a ledge near the bottom, her face turned to the wind and rain. The lingering soreness of his injured leg made the muddy descent less than comfortable, and his mood was grim by the time he reached the ledge.

"Cassie?"

"What do you want?" she asked without opening her eyes.

Jake prayed for patience as he crouched next to her. "Let's go up to the cottage. You're going to freeze out here."

"Would you stop acting all concerned and leave me alone?"

"I'm not acting anything."

Cassie hunched her shoulders and stared out at the water. Her rigid posture announced she wasn't feeling reasonable, and any attempt to make her reasonable was going to backfire.

"Come on, Cazz, let's go."

"Don't call me that."

Ah, hell. Jake knew she didn't like that nickname when she was angry; he'd just forgotten. "Look, come up to the cottage. I'll fix you a hot drink and we'll talk."

"I want to be left alone," she enunciated carefully.

"Then be alone in the cottage and not on this Godforsaken beach!"

"You can't order me around."

"I wasn't trying."

"Yes, you were." Cassie had taken all she could. No one was going to push her around now.

"Cassie, please."

"Give me a break. You said it yourself—you're just a stranger." She glared at him, torn between two needs: one, to be left alone; the other, to be touched and reminded about life.

"Damn it. It's my fault. If I hadn't upset you so much, you wouldn't be down here at all."

"That's conceited nonsense," Cassie snapped. "I'm responsible for my own actions. I don't need you. I've managed for a long time without your help—I can survive the next hour." She swung her legs off the ledge, too upset to think clearly. Jake's hand on her arm caught her off-balance, and they both tumbled to the sand a few feet below. He cussed furiously.

"I didn't ask for any help," she reminded, trying to rise from her sprawled position across his chest. "I said to leave me alone."

"I'm not going anywhere. Are you hurt?"

"No!" she shouted back.

And kissed him.

For a minute Jake was too busy returning her kiss to say anything. Then he flipped and neatly landed her below him. He thrust the aching part of his body against her thigh. "Well, I'm hurting a lot. Right here. And I've been hurting there for days."

Cassie gasped, feeling a sudden burst of warmth between her legs at his blatant movement. Despite the wind and cold, the heat of him burned her. It felt so right. So necessary.

He kissed her lightly, then ran the tip of his tongue down her throat. The neckline of her sweater stretched when he tugged, exposing her shoulder and the curve of her breasts. The warmth of his breath curled across her skin, while his teeth nipped the crest of one nipple. He caught her delicately through the cotton knit, exerting just enough pressure to give the greatest pleasure.

Dear heaven. Cassie's breathing became erratic. Jake slid the soft material of her sweater up over her stomach and gently cupped one swollen breast in his hand. He traced the silk line of her bra, teasing her without deepening the caress.

"Jake," she moaned.

He delayed another agonizing moment, gently nipping at her neck, then slid his finger beneath the silk barrier, exposing her breasts to his touch.

Cassie arched upward. His finger was hard and callused and it felt like heaven and hell combined. Jake bent his head, and his tongue caressed her firm nipples. Cassie's body shifted and rocked, reaching for him, welcoming the fire he was building in her blood.

"Is this what we were fighting about?" he breathed.

"Partly," she managed to choke.

"I'm tired of wondering if it's good or bad," he said fiercely. "I want you."

I want you. The words echoed in Cassie's head. There was no denying the passionate response of her body, begging for release. The heavy, needful throb in her abdomen was unbearable. She closed her eyes. Everything was so muddled, nothing clear the way it had been a week ago—decisions made, plans set in motion and no complications.

He released her from the enticing torment, raising his hand to brush tendrils of hair from her cheeks. "Let me be with you tonight."

She smiled sadly. "You mean *just* tonight, don't you? No commitments, no promises, and brand-new condoms."

"I won't give you a baby," Jake said honestly, though he wanted to. His body kept screaming that it was so very right, and then a little piece of them both would be created. Making a baby with Cassie would probably be the most exciting moment in his life. It appealed to a dark, primitive urge to brand her as his. Yet nothing was that simple. No matter how much Cassie intended to raise the baby on her own, he'd feel responsible, *committed,* unable to just walk away from either one.

No.

He wouldn't get her pregnant. And the really sticky part about the whole thing was that he didn't want anyone else getting her pregnant. Not even a nameless donor from a sperm bank.

Ah, hell. The wind kept blowing, and they were getting wet. Yet if anything, his desire had reached new heights just looking at her. Everything was gray, robbed of color by the storm—everything except Cassie. The rain had drenched them both, but she sat up, a graceful flower on the sand, and swayed with the wind.

"I'm cold," she whispered.

Jake leaned forward, catching her hands in his own and pulling her to her feet. "It's warm in the cottage... let's go up," he said gently. "I'd carry you, but we might both land in the hospital." She nodded, wrapping the excess folds of her skirt in her fist. The long length of her exposed thigh made Jake gulp. "Hurry," he implored.

She looked at him over her shoulder. "It isn't—oops!" She slipped against him. Jake grabbed an exposed tree root and scrambled for footing. "Sorry," she said breathlessly when their downward descent had been halted.

Cassie was plastered to him, her long legs wrapped around one of his thighs. "My pleasure," he said in a husky drawl.

Slowly, torturously she rubbed her abdomen against his arousal. Jake groaned. The heavy-lidded look to her eyes tempted him to forget the cold storm and their precarious, slippery location.

"I need a bath," she murmured. "And so do you." She touched a streak of mud on his cheek, trailing her fingernail down and catching the stubble of his late-afternoon beard.

"We could conserve water by sharing," he suggested.

She blinked. "I don't think so."

"You don't know what you're missing."

The sensuous expression faded from her face, leaving a wistful regret in its place. "Probably not." She lifted her chin. "But I'm not going to find out."

Dizzy at how close she'd come to relenting, Cassie turned and began to climb. Several times Jake put his palm on her behind and pushed, and even through the folds of sodden fabric she felt his burning, lingering handprint. At the top he winked, too obviously aware of the effect his touch had on her. "Stop it, O'Connor," she groused.

"I didn't say anything."

"You didn't have to."

Just then a fresh crash of thunder shook the ground, bringing with it another deluge of rain. Cassie turned and ran for the cottage with Jake close behind. They burst through the back door, spraying water and filth across the kitchen floor.

"Ugh," she said. "It's freezing in here. That furnace must be broken again."

"I'll check it. In the meantime, go take your bath while the water's still hot," Jake urged. "We may lose the electricity because of the storm."

"That's okay. You should go home and change."

His grin was boyishly impudent. "I'd rather stay. If I can't join you, at least I can listen and apply my imagination. Do you use bubble bath?"

"You're impossible," she informed him, at the same time deciding not to argue. "Just do me a favor...stay downstairs."

He held up his hand as though making a scout's pledge.
"My word of honor."

Cassie squished up the back staircase, unsure if she
wanted Jake to keep his word. She dropped her skirt over
the hamper to dry, and her hands were on the hem of the
sweater when she heard him "*da da-ing*" a striptease cho-
rus from the kitchen.

"Shut up," she yelled.

"Was that your sweater or the skirt?" he yelled back.

"None of your business."

"Spoilsport."

It was impossible to stay angry. Shivering, Cassie grabbed
a towel and stepped into the bathroom. The old mirror gave
back a wavy reflection, yet somehow it emphasized the way
the cotton knit clung to her breasts, her nipples standing out
in stark relief. She might as well have been naked.

Had Jake noticed?

The cheerful "da da-ing" still came from the kitchen, and
Cassie grinned in resignation.

Of course Jake had noticed.

The mournful sob of a foghorn worked its way into Cassie's consciousness, and she snuggled deeper into her pillow. She loved foghorns . . . loved the mystery and magic of
their lament cutting through the night.

It was dark, the storm pounding the coast with relentless
force, but through the fury of the wind she could hear the
ceaseless crash of breakers on the shore. There was a reassuring constancy about the ocean. Come what may, trage-
dies and triumphs, the waves would continue to curl into the
beach. Sometimes slow and gentle, sometimes frenzied and
angry, but they would still come.

When Jake was so persistent, he reminded her of ocean
waves. He had a way of digging in and refusing to leave—
like earlier that evening. She'd convinced him to go home
and change into dry clothes, but he'd come right back to
work on the recalcitrant furnace. They'd ended up spend-

ing the evening together, and then he'd fallen asleep on the couch. No amount of coaxing had awakened the man.

"Oh, well," Cassie murmured to herself. Turning onto her back, she yawned.

Just as she began to fall asleep again, a garbled curse rose through the cottage.

Jake.

Cassie stretched and reached for her robe. She walked down the stairs and peered into the living room, which was dimly lit by the coals on the hearth. He was still on the couch, but the quilt she'd covered him with lay in a crumpled heap on the floor.

This is good practice, she told herself, retrieving the quilt. *It's like having a child. They kick the blankets off … mom covers them up again. Simple.*

All at once Cassie gulped, realizing it wasn't so simple. Along with the quilt, Jake had also shucked his clothes; except for a pair of dark-colored briefs, he was nude. A little guiltily she stared at the shadowed planes of his body, tension curling inside her stomach. He was unlike any man she'd ever known, exuding a frank masculinity that compelled her senses and demanded an elemental response.

The floor was strewn with various articles of clothing, as though he'd flung them off without ever awakening. Cassie pulled the quilt over him again, then tearing her gaze away, she collected his shirt and jeans, neatly folding them. She sat in the rocking chair and tucked her cold feet beneath her, smiling wryly. Virgie would be certain Cassie and her son had slept together. She'd probably be planning a baby—or even wedding—shower before the day was out.

The dying coals from the fire popped and crackled while Cassie rocked and thought. Jake shifted restlessly, muttering, held in the grip of a dark dream.

"Jake?" Cassie whispered finally.

He didn't awaken, but for a moment he seemed to become more calm. She uncurled herself from the rocker and went to him. Beneath her comforting fingers she felt tense, knotted muscles.

"Jake?"

A shuddering sigh answered her.

"It's all right," she whispered, stroking his face and shoulders.

Abruptly Jake's arm clamped around her waist. He spun with her onto the floor, knocking the air from her lungs. Her robe flew open, and their bare legs tangled together.

"You rat," she sputtered, fuming at his duplicity and pushing at him. The heat from his body was an appealing contrast to the chill floor beneath her hips, a fact she didn't want to think about as she wriggled, attempting to escape.

"Cover them," he cried in a commanding tone of voice edged with worry.

Cassie froze, realizing Jake wasn't really awake.

"Damned sightseers." This time he didn't sound worried—just angry.

"Jake...it's over now. You're home," she said soothingly. "It's okay."

After several long moments his weight slid from her body. Cassie drew a shaky breath, unsure if she was more upset over Jake's nightmare or the erotic feel of him lying full length on top of her.

"I'm glad that's over," she murmured. Only it wasn't over, because Jake was just as deeply asleep as before.

With a judicious amount of tugging and cajoling, she managed to get him back on the couch. He was still restless. Twice he muttered a name, yet she couldn't make it out. She thought it belonged to a woman.

Oh, Jake.

The sound of the foghorn drifted around her, melding with all the other sounds. In the renewed stillness of the room, Cassie let herself think what she hadn't dared feel.

I wish things could be different. I wish it was me you wanted in your dreams . . . the dreams you don't believe in.

Jake groaned. His neck hurt. His leg hurt. And his spine was never going to recover. He'd slept in some awful beds before, but none as bad as . . . hell, where was he?

Out of one eye he saw a spinning wheel. It looked familiar. All at once he bolted to his feet. The cottage. He was in Cassie's cottage. On the couch. It was morning.

He looked down. And his clothes were gone.

Actually they weren't gone; they were folded on a chair. He must have removed them during the night, but he'd certainly never folded anything in his sleep before. Which meant that Cassie . . . He smiled.

Sweet Cassie was a wonder. Beneath her demure, unrevealing clothing beat the heart of the most sensual woman he'd ever known. Although it wasn't going to do him much good, because she was also the most stubborn woman he'd ever met.

A voice murmured in the kitchen, followed by a light laugh. Jake grabbed his jeans and slid them on. Barefoot, he ambled into the room and saw Cassie kneeling on the floor with her back to him. The delicious aroma of coffee filled the air, making his mouth water.

"All right now?" he heard her croon.

"I feel great," Jake said, amused. "But you're talking to yourself." Cassie jumped and landed on her derriere. At the same time a small animal streaked across the floor with a startled hiss. "Sorry," he apologized, helping her to her feet. "I didn't mean to surprise you."

"That's okay." She rubbed her rear end.

Jake's eyes darkened. "Let me do that."

"Uh—uh." Cassie backed away.

"I was just offering some tender loving care."

"Uh-huh," she muttered again. "And what else?"

"Sweetheart, I'm devastated. I don't know why you're so suspicious." Jake hooked his thumbs in his belt loops and grinned. "Bet I could make your bottom feel better... lots better."

A smile twitched at the corner of her mouth. "Since I'm living next to your mother, I think we should make some ground rules."

His eyebrows raised. "Such as?"

"Such as keeping our hands to ourselves."

He clucked and shook his head. "In that case, I hope you kept your hands to yourself last night. There I was, dead to the world... at your complete mercy. Did you behave yourself?" To Jake's utter amazement, Cassie's face turned a delicate pink. "Incredible," he declared. "You had your wicked way with me, didn't you?"

"I didn't do anything like... well... *that*," she denied heatedly. "You were having a nightmare. I tried to help."

His grin wavered. "Oh, that," he said. "It's nothing."

"But—"

"Nothing," Jake insisted. He didn't want to discuss his infrequent nightmares with Cassie. They were part of his life. The ugly part. The part filled with demands and pressures, where he had to fight not only the cold ruthlessness of criminals and fanatics, but also against the cost-saving measures that jeopardized human lives.

"Sure." Cassie's face was skeptical. "It's nothing. Anyway, have some coffee." She motioned him to the table, where he had the distinct impression she'd rather pour the hot liquid over his head than in his cup.

"Er... by the way, who's your visitor?" Jake asked, nodding to the cat crouching in the corner, its wary gaze fixed on him.

Cassie's expression softened. "I found him under a bush by the door. He was soaking wet and half-starved, poor thing. It took me forever to coax him inside."

"At least you didn't have to coax me inside."

"Right. You barged in."

Jake sighed. Nothing about Cassie was easy. He could spend his entire life trying to figure her out. "You know, I'm in town for another three weeks. We could ... get to know each other," he said suggestively.

She looked at him and smiled evenly. "Jake, I told you I wasn't going to carry on an affair. I have other plans. I'm going to have a baby."

He slammed his cup down so hard the steaming liquid slopped over the sides. "Quit reminding me of that!"

"God," Cassie moaned. She sank into a chair, putting her elbows on the table and her face in her hands. "We don't have anything in common. We want different things and different places. Having an affair won't change that."

"I wasn't—"

"You hate small towns and kids."

Jake grabbed what was left of his coffee. Caffeine, he needed caffeine to get through this discussion, because Cassie was driving him crazy. "I don't dislike small towns." *Not really.*

"And you're violently against marriage," she continued as though he hadn't spoken.

Although she'd said it in an entirely philosophical way, Jake glared. "That's right, I'm against marriage. But I wasn't always. Christine and I got married a few years after college. I thought she was wonderful. I knew she'd run around a lot, even when we were seeing each other, but I thought that ended when we got engaged. Boy, I had a lot of faith back then."

"Oh."

"Yeah, oh," he repeated curtly. "About eight months after the wedding I was sent to Saudi Arabia for a job. Christine didn't want to come and she resented my going. When I got back I found out she was pregnant. With someone else's baby."

A soft gasp escaped Cassie's throat.

"It didn't take long to find out she'd been unfaithful from the very beginning. Hell, she probably had sex with the bellhop on our wedding night."

Cassie flinched. "It must have been awful."

"I survived."

"Did you?"

"What's that supposed to mean?" A stab of remorse struck Jake at the sight of her pale face; she hadn't done anything to deserve his attack. "Never mind," he said, touching her cheek. "I'm sorry, I didn't mean to spout off like that. You should have just hauled off and hit me."

She lifted her chin. "Actually I was just deciding between a right or left hook."

"Could you warn me ahead of time?" he asked, beginning to smile. "So I'll know which way to duck."

"Then I'd lose my advantage."

His gaze was warm as he looked her up and down. "I—ouch!" Jake leapt to his feet, and the cat—who had been trying to climb his leg—darted away with a hiss. "What does he want?"

Cassie put out her hand, and after a few seconds of deliberation the cat sidled over and rubbed her arm. A loud purr rumbled from its chest. "Just a little attention," she murmured. "Maybe some more food and a warm place to sleep."

With the cat lolling and purring indecently in her arms, Cassie walked to the refrigerator and removed a bowl of boneless chicken. The feline perked his ears and was quite content to perch on her lap while she fed him scraps. Jake tried not to feel jealous. It was deflating to realize he'd instantly trade places with a scruffy, half-starved cat who didn't have sense to come out of the rain.

"There, now," she crooned, scratching under the animal's chin. The long, rumpled fur was drying into distinctive silver tabby markings. "You act like you haven't eaten in a month." One of his paws wrapped around her wrist while she caressed him, and his almond-shaped eyes closed in ecstasy.

Just then Jake's stomach growled. "I'm starved, too," he said mournfully. "Aren't I worth feeding?"

"Sorry, I got distracted. There's some scrambled eggs and bacon in the pan and biscuits warming in the oven."

Jake grumbled under his breath all the while he was serving himself. He envied a damned cat. His friends would laugh themselves silly.

Taking a lock of her hair, Cassie waved the ends in the feline's face. He lazily swiped at the shiny strands. "I don't think he belongs to anyone," she said softly. "Virgie doesn't have any pets, and there aren't a lot of houses in this direction."

"Somebody probably dumped him," Jake commented, sitting down again. It was the cynical truth. People were always dumping things they didn't want, things that had become inconvenient or a problem. Why quibble about a cat?

"I'll ask around. Maybe I can keep him."

"He seems pretty content." *My God, why are we talking about stray pets? Why can't you look at me with calculating eyes, so I can pretend you're like every other marriage-minded female I've known?*

"I've been thinking about getting a dog," Cassie said. "Maybe a golden retriever or a collie. Do you think Virgie would mind?"

Mind? Jake figured his mother would let Cassie do anything she pleased to keep her from moving. "Sure," he said carelessly. "Why not?" *Why can't you be happy with a dog, rather than a baby?*

Jake pushed at the food on his plate, suddenly losing his appetite. Cassie was right: they were worlds apart. He was too cynical, too distrustful for her kind of gentleness. Even if he could learn to have confidence in the vows a man and woman made in marriage, he could never be the kind of man she needed. All he would end up doing was destroying the natural innocence that so appealed to him.

Chapter Seven

Virgie was sitting in the living room, looking at photo albums, when Jake returned to the house. He expected an interrogation, or at least a comment about the night he'd spent at Cassie's, but she just sat there, turning the pages and looking innocent.

"Okay," he said, unable to stand the anticipation. "Just ask. I know you want to know about Cassie and me."

"If I was going to say anything, I'd say leave her alone," Virgie said slowly. "My plan was to have you donate sperm for her baby. I don't want Cassie hurt. You aren't the right man for her."

Jake already knew that; he'd told himself the same thing a hundred times. Still, it was new and more painful to hear his own mother repeat the truth. "Out of... idle curiosity, why not?"

"Do you really need me to explain?"

No, he didn't. He was selfish and inconsiderate, cynical and worlds too hard. But that didn't stop him from wanting Cassie Cavannaugh with every breath he took. "She doesn't play games. She's completely honest and so damned baffling I don't know which end is up."

"And?"

"And she wants marriage and babies and to live in this little town on the edge of nowhere." Even Jake could hear the edge in his tone. "She wants fairy tales and myths."

"Does she?"

"Hell, Mother, you know what she wants."

"Maybe a little. Like you once said, she's very private."

Jake rubbed his forehead and tried to think rationally. "She's a dreamer."

"A realistic dreamer. It's not the same."

At the moment he wasn't sure. It had been so long since he'd dreamed, forever since he'd believed in anything. Everything about Cassie was a contradiction, nothing black-and-white. Realistic dreamer? What a fitting paradox.

"Mom...yesterday...you said something that bothered me. Something about the ocean not killing her before.... What did you mean?" For an endless moment he waited, dreading the answer yet needing to know.

Finally she sighed, staring at the album in her lap. "Her parents drowned when she was nine."

"What happened to Cassie?" he asked harshly.

"Steve and Derrick were at camp. The rest of the family went out on the water—to go whale watching, I think. When the boat went down, Cassie was the only one wearing a life jacket. It's really quite remarkable. She was all alone, miles out to sea, and yet she survived."

All alone.

Alone.

What other secrets did Cassie's eyes hold? Was this the real reason she spent hours absorbed by the rhythms of the ocean, wading in the icy rush of the waves? Was she searching for an answer to her parents' deaths? An explanation for a tragedy an adult would have trouble understanding, much less a child? He'd blithely assumed he'd seen the real Cassie, that he'd glimpsed her deepest soul and se-

crets—a lovely woman with passionate dreams and endur-
ing innocence. But he hadn't seen her at all.

A woman knows when a man's eyes dismiss her.

I never dismissed you.

Hadn't he? Hadn't he been trying to do that from the first
moment they met, boxing her into untidy packages of assumption and contradiction?

"I don't understand her," Jake said slowly.

Virgie's smile was almost imperceptible. "Few people do.
We all adore her, but there's something about Cassie that's
different. Most people try to pretend it isn't there. You could
try to accept her."

He rubbed his temples. "I thought you didn't want us involved."

"When was the last time you listened to me?"

"You're still matchmaking," Jake accused, but without
his usual heat. "You and Cassie are something else. You
want us together, and she's holding me at arm's length."

"I'm not matchmaking," his mother retorted. "*If* things
were different, *if* you were compatible, *if* you wanted some
of the same things, then she'd be the perfect daughter-in-
law. But 'if' doesn't matter. As for being involved...I sus-
pect it's too late to be worried about that."

"We're not sleeping together," Jake disclaimed, as
though he hadn't resorted to every wile he possessed to get
Cassie Cavannaugh into bed with him.

Virgie looked at her son sternly. "I'm not an idiot. In the
modern world, sex doesn't necessarily mean involvement.
I'm talking about something else. You've never had trouble keeping away from a woman before."

Impossible. His mother was utterly impossible. She was
also right. There was a world of difference between acting
on a basic need and making love. With Cassie it would be
making love, not just having sex. And it had never been that
way, not even with his ex-wife.

Abruptly a cold sweat broke out on Jake's back. It was alarming, *damned* alarming, if he was thinking in those terms. Somehow he had to get a grip on himself.

Leaning over, he picked up a stack of photo albums from the coffee table. "Do any of these have a picture of Cassie?" he asked, not even trying to sound casual.

She gave him a long, calculating look. "Quite a few. I've known her for a long time."

Jake tucked the books under his arm and headed for his bedroom. He had some thinking to do. Maybe if he could look at a picture instead of the real woman, he'd be able to see more clearly.

Cassie looked down at her toes and wiggled them against the bed sheets. Maybe she should paint her toenails red. Fire-engine red. *No.* She wanted to do something reckless and defiant, but a pedicure didn't qualify.

It had been five days since she'd caught more than a glimpse of Jake. He was doing a far better job of avoiding her than she'd done of avoiding him. But why was he avoiding her?

It has to be sex. He was sulking because she wouldn't go to bed with him.

Maybe it isn't just sex.

Like a Ping-Pong ball going back and forth in her head, Cassie debated the issue. She didn't have a reason for wanting to see Jake. After all, she'd made up her mind. Having an affair would just complicate things.

"Like it wasn't complicated enough," she muttered.

Cassie sighed, thinking about Jake's anger and pain...the betrayal he'd suffered because of a woman named Christine. She could see him in her imagination—an eager, idealistic young man in love for the first time. An unfamiliar, primitive emotion rose in Cassie. She wanted to smack Christine silly. No wonder talk of a baby upset Jake so much. No wonder he despised the thought of marriage, believing it was doomed to failure. From the moment he'd told her about his ex-wife, any lingering wishful thought of a future with him had vanished.

Cassie looked out the window, watching a boat bob on the ocean. It was going to be a lovely day. Perfect for sailing or picnics. . . . All at once she smiled. There were more ways than one of getting a man's attention. Sympathy aside, Jake had ruined her peace of mind—he deserved a little retaliation.

Sliding from the bed, Cassie dressed in a pair of well-worn jeans and a camisole top. At the last moment she threw on an old bomber jacket, letting it hang open to expose the lacy garment beneath. Jake didn't like the clothing she normally wore? Let him get a load of this!

With a hammer in one hand and a toolbox in the other, she walked jauntily out onto the deck.

"Nice day," she said to herself, taking a deep breath.

The storm had passed, leaving the air freshly washed and the sky clear. The ocean sparkled in the sunlight, and there was the piercing sound of gulls crying as they swooped and dived in search of breakfast. The breeze was warm, so Cassie removed the jacket and draped it across a railing. Then she knelt and started using the hammer for all it was worth.

Jake woke up feeling as if he were suffering from a hangover . . . when he hadn't enjoyed the dubious pleasure of getting drunk. He also felt like a coward. For days he'd pored over his mother's photo albums like a thief searching for a diamond. Each photo of Cassie revealed something different—something unique. He loved her eyes in those pictures. They dominated, with an endlessly fascinating array of emotions.

The early pictures showed a young, coltish girl with eyes too big for her face. The slender girl of those shots had matured into a slim-hipped, full-bodied shapeliness. Her eyes were more mysterious now in their fey expressions, but they still reflected innocence. And paradoxically a genuine honesty.

"Ugh." Jake ran his fingers through his hair, making the ends stick up in shaggy spikes. About then he realized the constant tap-tap-tapping he heard wasn't a headache demanding attention but a hammer pounding on nails.

Nails? He yawned and frowned, not particularly concerned. Who was working so early in the morning? It took another ten seconds for the realization to explode in his mind before he hopped out of bed, cursing a blue streak.

"Damn-fool woman—can't leave her alone for a minute," he growled, yanking a pair of denims from their roost on the bureau. He conveniently discounted the fact that he'd ignored her for several days.

A second later he nearly toppled on his face when he tried to shove both feet down the same pant leg. He yanked the zipper up and stormed through the house. His mother raised a cup of tea at him as he passed. Wisely she didn't say a word.

"What do you think you're doing?" he shouted at Cassie, his heart in his throat, as she straddled one of the cross beams. There was nothing but empty air and a thirty-foot drop below her.

"Rebuilding my deck," she said sweetly.

"That's my job!"

"Could have fooled me."

"Cassie, get the hell off that beam," he warned.

Her lips pursed. "No, I don't think so." Setting the claw portion of the hammer around the rusty head of an old nail, she started yanking.

Jake gulped, hardly able to breathe. He suddenly realized he'd been wrong about the Cavannaugh brothers. They obviously knew Cassie needed a keeper, no matter how much she resented their interference. Those good old boys deserved medals for their patience, and he felt a fierce glow of sympathy for their years of dealing with this woman who was *utterly impossible*.

It was bad enough that she was risking life and limb. Did she have to look so sexy while she was doing it? Her hair was a silky cloud around her head and shoulders, and she was wearing tight jeans and a scanty top. Very scanty. His blood pressure was ready to explode, especially when he saw the darker aureoles of her nipples strain against the sheer fabric, tightened by the brush of cool morning air.

He walked across the deck, fists clenching and unclenching. "I said, *get the hell off*." Without another word he pulled her from the beam and dragged her into the cottage.

It occurred to him that his actions were hardly nineties behavior, but that didn't seem to make a difference. He was sure—nearly sure—that Cassie had deliberately provoked him. His gentle temptress had claws? Well, he had muscles and he wasn't going to let her risk breaking her neck to make a point.

Aside from an initial gasp, she was also remarkably silent as he dragged her up the stairs, so he didn't know what to expect when he tossed her on the bed. The cat she'd adopted hissed and dove off the quilted coverlet, up the curtains and onto a tall armoire in the corner. Baleful eyes peered over the edge, and the tip of a tail flicked the air.

Jake ignored the feline and planted his hands on his hips, glaring. For a minute Cassie just lay there, her enigmatic eyes intent. "Well?" he demanded. He expected all hell to break loose when she got her breath back; he knew she hated being ordered around.

Cassie tried to keeping from laughing. Jake looked like a wild cowboy with his morning beard and bare chest. He also looked like a belligerent little boy caught with his fingers in the candy dish.

"Well what?"

"Aren't you going to yell at me?"

She lifted one eyebrow. "I'll think about it."

"It isn't safe out there," he argued despite her apparent lack of resistance. "You pushed me too far."

"Did I?"

"You know you did," Jake snapped. He took several deep breaths, trying to control himself. There was one argument that might work on Cassie. "How can you have a baby if you're dead?" he asked.

"You don't want me to have a baby."

"That isn't the issue."

Her expression shifted subtly. "Really?"

"No," he exploded. "I just don't want you working on that deck. I'll finish it myself."

"That's interesting," she said reflectively, as though she didn't really believe him. "You know . . . you'd be almost perfect if you weren't such a tyrannical, opinionated, domineering caveman. I could endure your other faults, but those are impossible."

His jaw sagged and he stared at her, speechless.

Cassie stretched slowly, loving the way his gaze followed the arching movement of her body and lingered on the deep valley between her breasts. Their relationship had enhanced the sensual side of her nature. Poor man—if he still thought of her as a shy, small-town spinster, he had a shock coming.

"Cassie?"

She smiled slowly at him. "Yes?" She ran the tip of her tongue over her lips . . . just for effect. From the sudden tension in Jake's body and his pained expression, she decided it had been effective. Just as he was reaching for her, she neatly slid off the bed, evading his arms.

Jake fell on the mattress, groaning. "Cassie," he protested. "That isn't fair."

"You're on vacation, pal, so vacate."

"Those words don't have any relation to one another," he protested. His large hand grabbed the comforter and pulled it over him. "I'm tired. You woke me up early. I deserve a little tender loving care."

"Poor baby," she crooned sympathetically. "In that case I'll leave you alone to get some rest."

"But I don't want to be—"

The door closing behind her cut off his words. Cassie grinned. She ran down to the kitchen, humming softly. She figured it wouldn't take long for Jake to get bored with the empty bedroom.

It didn't.

Ten minutes later he came stomping downstairs, muttering to himself.

"I called and took a few days off from the center," she said cheerfully. "We're going on a picnic."

"No, we're not."

"Wanna bet?"

No, Jake didn't want to make a bet. He recognized the mulish determination in Cassie's face. For some reason she was determined they have a picnic. So they'd have a picnic.

"I have to take a shower," he said, trying to stall.

"You have fifteen minutes," Cassie informed him. She didn't look up as he reluctantly departed. She quickly finished packing the ingredients of their picnic lunch and walked out onto the repaired portion of the deck, breathing in the fresh air. "Beautiful," she murmured.

It seemed a good day for wandering the coast, and the weather was favoring them with sunshine and clear skies—a late Indian summer. If she couldn't make love with Jake, at least she'd have this memory.

Though Cassie had specified fifteen minutes, almost a half hour passed before Jake returned. "You're hell on my best intentions, Miss Cavannaugh," he said resignedly, wrapping his arms around her. "Brr," he growled.

She leaned back against him, enjoying the strength of his body. "Why are you so cold?"

"I was forced to take a cold shower . . . my pants were too tight."

A smile tugged at Cassie's mouth. "Too tight, huh?"

"Definitely too tight." Jake nuzzled her shoulder with his lips. "You smell good," he whispered. "Like ripe peaches." The tip of his tongue traced the scant camisole straps, and she obligingly turned her head to allow him greater access. "You also taste good," he added thickly.

"I like that," Cassie breathed. Sensations of hot and cold raced alternately through her blood from the velvet slide of his tongue. "But you should stop...or else that cold shower will be for nothing."

"It's already too late." Jake's hand flattened on her abdomen, pressing her against his hips. "See what I mean?"

Cassie did...or rather she *felt* what Jake meant. She would have been flattered by his urgent reaction if she hadn't been aching so much herself. For an instant her eyes closed, and the world spun in a lazy circle.

"We...uh...we should go," she murmured.

Jake sighed into Cassie's hair, holding her a second longer. "Okay. Let's get on with your picnic," he said, his voice husky.

Smiling but not saying anything, Cassie prodded him back into the house, where they collected the various picnic items she'd prepared.

"Can't we have some coffee first?" Jake pleaded as she locked the front door.

"Later."

"You're a hard-hearted lady."

"Nonsense, I'm very sweet. I'll even do the driving since you're so tired. Just give me the keys." Cassie held out her hand.

"Uh-uh!" Jake stepped back, waving his keys in the air. "This is my 'Beamer,' my baby—you don't get to touch."

"It's just a car."

He patted the gleaming hood of his BMW. "Don't worry, darling, she doesn't understand. She's—"

"Don't you dare say I'm only a woman."

Jake looked at Cassie's mock-angry expression. "Right. I wouldn't *dare*."

"Don't dare think it, either."

"I...never mind." With exaggerated courtesy he opened the passenger side of the vehicle and helped her into the seat. He even tried to help with the seat belt, but she slapped his hands away when they drifted into unlikely territory. "You're no fun," he complained.

"Your idea of fun is always the same thing. I thought men matured out of the groping stage after they turned thirty."

"Ouch. And here I thought it was a compliment." Jake settled into the driver's seat and started the engine. "Where to?" he asked.

"Stop by the senior center first, okay?"

He groaned. "I thought you took some time off."

"I did, but I'm working on a funding request to increase our meal program for low-income seniors. It needs to be mailed today."

"I thought you just organized crafts and games," Jake commented.

Cassie's head snapped around. "I do a hell of a lot more than that. Fund-raising can be a full-time job alone, but I also plan trips, do a monthly newsletter, conduct specialized driver's training for seniors, organize health fairs, recruit—"

"Sorry," he interrupted hastily. "I didn't mean to suggest you didn't earn your salary."

Jake followed Cassie into the center when they arrived, then promptly wished he hadn't. A barrage of eyes was fixed on the two of them. Some hopeful, some speculative and all of them curious.

"Morning, Cassie," a woman with blue hair called out.

Blue? Jake looked more carefully. Yes, it was blue. It was definitely blue. "Is she the geriatric version of a punk rocker?" he whispered in Cassie's ear.

"Shh," she hissed, but the corners of her mouth trembled. "Good morning, Phyllis…everyone. I'm taking a few days off, so check with Virgie if you need anything." With Jake's hand pushing at her back, she went into her office. He leaned against the door and began laughing.

"How come blue?"

She put her hands on her hips and tried to look stern. "White hair sometimes turns yellow, so she uses a blue rinse to get rid of it. She's a very nice lady."

"With psychedelic hair." Jake peered through the large interior windows that gave Cassie a full view of the recreation room. There was no privacy in her office, none at all. The seniors were unashamedly curious and stared right back at him. "I wish you had some curtains in here," he complained.

Sorting a file on her desk, Cassie didn't look up. "Whatever for?"

"What do you think?"

This time she looked at him, and the invitation in his face was unmistakable. "You wouldn't."

"I would."

Cassie thought for a moment, then shook her head in exasperation. "You're unbelievable. Your mother is out there."

"And every senior citizen from Sandpiper Cove," Jake agreed, resigned. "Kind of cramps my style."

"We're going for a drive." Cassie folded several sheets of paper into an envelope, which she dropped into her Out basket. The postman would collect it when he delivered the center's mail. "And a picnic. Let's go."

"Your wish is my command."

"I doubt that," she murmured absently. When they got into the car again she told Jake to go south on Highway 101. From a satchel at her feet she produced a thermos and two no-spill travel mugs. The fragrant scent of coffee mixed with orange and cinnamon filled the air, and Jake's stomach rumbled. Lord, what she did to the humble coffee bean was nothing short of a miracle. He accepted a cup and took a deep, burning swallow. The hot liquid hit his stomach and started to reverse the icy process his cold shower had begun.

After another moment she unwrapped some food and held it out. Jake put his mug on the dashboard and took the offering. A brief glance told him it was a kind of turnover, stuffed with ham, cheese and mushrooms. "This looks great. When did you have time to make it?"

Cassie shrugged. "I pulled them out of the freezer and zapped them in the microwave. Eat up, there's plenty more."

Never one to hold back when good food was offered, Jake cheerfully munched down three of the turnovers. He was afraid he'd turn into a balloon if he stayed around Cassie for long. Though slender herself, she fed the people around her with generous, loving hands.

"So, where are we going?" he asked as he polished off a second cup of coffee. With food and java filling his stomach, he didn't mind the early morning, though he still regretted the loss of Cassie in his arms.

"To see *Darlingtonias*." Cassie grinned at his blank look. "Actually we're going to see the bogs where they grow. Being October, they're not especially active."

"Bogs? Active? Are we talking animal, vegetable or mineral?"

"Vegetable, though they can act like animals."

"You're deliberately confusing me," he accused.

She laughed and took the cup he was waving at her. "*Darlingtonias* are also called pitcher plants, and they eat insects, like the Venus's-flytrap. Actually," she mused, "they're really quite ugly... but fascinating."

Skepticism was one of Jake's talents, so he wagged a skeptical finger in Cassie's direction. "I don't buy a word of it. That type of plant grows in tropical climates. Not in rainy Oregon."

"Since when did you become a botanist?" she challenged.

"About the same time you did."

"Shows how much you know—I majored in social sciences in college but I minored in botany—along with meteorology."

Jake had the grace to look abashed. "Sorry. I accept your word that such a plant exists. And I withdraw any comments I might have recently made about the weather."

"Smart."

"Was that a reference to my mind or my apology?" he queried innocently.

"You don't want to know."

But she was wrong. Jake wanted to know *everything* about what Cassie was thinking and feeling—he just had the good sense not to push. He hoped.

Having fed them both, Cassie kicked off her sneakers and tucked her feet beneath her in the seat, then had to endure Jake's humorous glance. Leaning closer, she slid her hand onto his thigh and rested it there. She felt calm, peaceful, like the quiet before a storm. It didn't matter that the storm was coming; you simply accepted what was offered.

The *Darlingtonia Botanical Wayside* was a favorite place of Cassie's. Just north of Florence, a trail wandered through thickets of bushes and trees and past the sphagnum bogs where the pitcher plants grew. It was only a short hike from beginning to end, and she expected some comment from Jake about driving almost two hours to see the place where an ugly plant grew when it wasn't winter.

They had the trail to themselves—few people bothered with the wayside in October. They paused on the wooden platform near one of the bogs and leaned over the railing while Cassie described the scene in spring and summer. To her surprise Jake listened to her descriptions with quiet attentiveness and seemed intrigued by the few stalks of seemingly lifeless growth.

There was a stillness to the bog, a sense of ageless waiting.

"I didn't know this place existed," Jake said when Cassie's voice drifted into silence. "It's a scene out of time." He was rewarded with her quick smile.

"Exactly, it's like catching a glimpse of the primeval past."

After a moment Jake shivered, reminded of another time and place. Two years before, he'd spent a week in the swamps and bayous of Louisiana. Then he'd only felt the eerie murkiness of the black water, the smell of rotting vegetation and the relentless weight of Creole lore and superstition.

All at once Cassie snuggled closer, warming him through the memories. He looked down and stroked the curve of her jaw.

"What are you thinking?" she whispered.

He shrugged. "The bayous of the South. They're sort of like this bog. I can almost envision fireflies and the gray mist of Spanish moss surrounding us at dusk."

Though Jake's voice was disdainful, a dreamy expression crossed Cassie's face. "I always wanted to visit the Deep South, especially New Orleans and the bayou country," she murmured, eyelids drooping as she imagined the distant places she had never seen. "Mysterious and magical. Do fireflies really sparkle?"

"They . . . flicker," Jake said, reluctant to take the whimsical happiness from Cassie's smile. "I didn't care for the swamps—they were grim and full of death."

"Life," she corrected gently.

"No, if you were there, you'd see how dismal they are."

Still smiling faintly, Cassie leaned away. Lifting a hand, she stroked the tense muscles in Jake's jaw. "Not dismal, just different. I can close my eyes and see it in my head. Cicadas calling, the cry of an egret echoing against the stillness, fox fire and fireflies glowing through the mist."

"Decay."

"A part of life. Destruction and rebirth can't be separated."

Jake wanted to cry out, to deny her words, yet he couldn't. His heart accepted what his mind could not. Cassie would have sensed what he'd missed in the swamps. Not the darkness, but the immediacy and intensity of life. He would give almost anything to see them through her eyes. To her, they would have been beautiful.

But he would never visit Louisiana with Cassie; he'd never go anywhere with her.

Oh, Cassie, why couldn't I have known you before I forgot how to hope?

Cassie dropped her head back to catch the slight warmth of the sun on her throat. A large log, polished from being tossed in the ocean and then discarded by the waves on the beach, provided support for her back. Jake was asleep, his head on her lap. Even slumber hadn't erased the troubled lines from his face.

What is wrong?

Nothing.

Why won't you talk to me?

I told you, nothing is wrong.

But Cassie knew there was a problem; she felt the pull of it on her shoulders and mind. The brightness of the waves and the laughter of children in the distance couldn't erase the sensation. Her fingers combed through Jake's dark hair, and he mumbled, a frown flitting across his mouth. Even on this sun-drenched beach he was restless, even in sleep.

Was it the same nightmare as before?

She continued to stroke his hair until he quieted into more tranquil slumber. Only then did she rest her head again on the tumbled drift log and close her eyes. Perhaps the picnic was a mistake, and Jake's protests about not wanting to go had been sincere. Yet that didn't explain the strange mood he had fallen into since visiting the Darlingtonia bog.

Maybe their discussion about the South was to blame. She frowned. Or maybe he was thinking about his ex-wife and the death of love and dreams. A heavy, shuddering sigh tore at Cassie's chest. He must have loved his ex-wife, deeply, completely. Some men loved that way only once. Yet a foolish woman, blind to his worth, had thrown it away.

For a fleeting moment Cassie let herself imagine what it would be like to have Jake's love. He would be demanding and impetuous and sometimes difficult to tolerate. He would often make her laugh, and then he'd make her so angry she couldn't see straight. And more than anything, he'd be wonderful.

"Stop it," she muttered. A man who'd reached the age of thirty-seven knew what he wanted and how to get it . . . and what he didn't want. Commitment and a family were two of his big "don't wants."

Two children raced across the beach, shouting and laughing as they chased their dog, who was chasing a sea gull. Cassie's mouth turned upward. So much joy and energy in such small packages. They seemed oblivious to the chill bite of October air and unaware of anything but the adventure of beachcombing and play.

As the dog zoomed past with the kids in close pursuit, Jake shifted, then yawned. "Cassie?"

The soft sound of her name, murmured in Jake's husky, sleepy voice, made her pulse skip. "Yes?"

"I'm hungry. Can we eat yet?"

The little-boy lament—uttered from such a wickedly adult male—made Cassie shake her head. "Of course," she said wryly. "I'll get the basket."

When she returned from the car, Jake grinned and stretched. He leaned against the drift log and extended his legs. "I feel better," he announced.

His switch of mood made Cassie dismiss her apprehensions. Maybe she'd been imagining a problem where one didn't exist—some men got awful grouchy when they were tired.

Jake foraged in the basket, nodding approval at the selection of food. "Chicken, salad...oh, good! Brownies and chocolate mousse." He removed the container and took a taste. "Yum, you know what I'd like to do with this?"

She refused to rise to his sensual, teasing bait. "Yes, eat it. With a spoon."

"Better." Jake leaned forward and whispered in her ear.

"Stop that!" Cassie pushed his wandering hands away. "We're out in public." She peeked to see if the children were still close by and breathed a sigh of relief when she spotted them a good distance down the beach.

"I know." Jake's tongue touched the curve of her neck. He whispered another suggestion. Cassie squirmed. Then he added a few embellishments, and in words made love to her right there on the sand.

Chapter Eight

On the drive home Cassie reclined in the seat and dozed, listening to a tape recording of a medieval flute composition. Jake had originally complained about playing the tape, then he'd conceded. His taste normally ran to jazz and the blues, but she suspected he was beginning to like her style of music, though he wouldn't admit it. Men could be very stubborn.

"Cassie?"

"Mmm?" She turned her head, yawning delicately.

"We're home."

"That's nice." Cassie closed her eyes again. A light, masculine laugh tickled her senses. All at once the cushioned car seat became an unstable world of air and rhythmic movement. Her eyes shot open, and she grabbed frantically at Jake's neck. "What are you doing?"

"Carrying you ... isn't that obvious?"

The only thing obvious to Cassie was that she was several feet off the ground. "Put me down. I'm too heavy for this."

He laughed again. "You don't weigh that much."

"I'm serious, you'll hurt your back." He ignored her protests and carried her through the door of the cottage, which apparently he'd had the forethought to open ahead of time. "You aren't listening to me." Secretly Cassie was a little glad he wasn't listening. She felt safe and happy being held by Jake.

"Hold on tight," he said, climbing the staircase.

"Famous last words," she teased when he stopped in the middle and shifted her weight.

"Brat." Jake dropped her on the bed in much the same way he'd done that morning, only this time he wasn't angry. He stood grinning at her, breathing easily despite having carried her from the car. "Someone should teach you respect."

"Oh? And who's going to do that?"

Jake put one knee on the mattress. "How about me?"

The look in his eyes was hot and exciting, causing Cassie's heart to skip a beat. Her resistance was wearing thin. In fact, it was practically nonexistent. He reached out a finger and traced her lips, then trailed it down her throat. For an endless moment he played with the ribbon lacing the edges of her camisole together.

"I've never known anyone like you," he whispered. "You're like a rainbow. Something I can see but can't touch."

"You're touching me now," she said with a husky laugh.

Jake shivered. Gently he tugged on the satin ribbon, freeing it from the top two holes. Her breasts swelled, separating the edges even more. She didn't do anything, just lay there, barely breathing. A trickle of sweat ran down his back as he pulled the ribbon free and dropped it off the edge of the bed.

Reaching out, he smoothed the fabric over her breast and felt an eager nipple nestle into his palm. "I thought—" Oh, hell, he didn't know what he thought anymore. He'd tried to stay away, telling himself it was the noble thing to do. The truth was, he was scared to death of Cassie Cavannaugh. In all the years since his divorce, no woman had tempted him like Cassie, no woman had touched his soul the way she did.

"*Cassie*." He wasn't even aware he'd spoken her name out loud until she stirred, stroking his cheek.

"I know," she whispered.

"Thank you for a beautiful day," he said softly. "I particularly enjoyed our conversation on the beach."

Her head shook. "You never stop."

"It's one of those 'guy' things. You enter puberty on hormonal overdrive, and it doesn't slow down until rigor mortis. Our only hope is to develop a little finesse along the way."

"Is that so?"

"Absolutely." Jake leaned over her. He ran his palms down her sides and curved them across her belly, then deliberately eased the zipper down on her jeans. Cassie's eyes were filled with mysterious emotions as they watched him slide the denims down her legs, but the response of her body wasn't hidden.

"That night," he whispered, never taking his gaze from the deep, silver-blue intensity of her gaze, "that first night you moved in, I wanted to touch you.... I wanted to know if you were as hot as you made me feel." Carefully he moved back up her abdomen and gently circled each nipple.

Cassie moaned. "How did you feel?"

"Like . . . like now. Empty, aching . . . angry."

"Angry?" His fingers moved in ever-widening circles, savouring the satiny feel of her.

"Angry that I responded. I didn't want to...I didn't even like you," she explained.

"I was angry *because* I liked you. Different sides of the same coin, I guess." Jake tugged teasingly at the silk-covered elastic of her panties. "I wish . . ." His words trailed off.

"We'd better stop," she whispered.

Jake closed his eyes tightly, but it didn't help. He could still see Cassie in front of him, her enticing body soft and responsive. Stopping would surely kill him. "But—"

"Think about it," she said, echoing what he'd said that first night on the beach. "Condoms aren't one hundred percent effective—sometimes they fail. Would you ever be really sure it wasn't your baby?"

Jake groaned and pulled away. Cassie was right. He couldn't be sure. He'd always wonder about the baby. Hell, the baby would drive him nuts. It was driving him nuts already and it hadn't even been conceived.

The phone rang, startling them both. He glanced at Cassie, who kept staring at the ceiling, a distant expression on her face. "Shall I get that?" he asked.

Cassie blinked. She wished life would give her a peaceful five minutes to figure things out. What demon of mischief had brought Jake into her life? He was so self-sufficient, so angry and hurting. The barriers he'd erected to keep people away also kept him inside. Alone. Separated, even from his family.

She couldn't let herself start imagining a future where there wasn't any. She wasn't even sure she wanted a future with Jake. She hovered between loving him and wanting to brain him for being so blind.

But did she love him?

Between the fourth and fifth ring from the telephone, Cassie decided she didn't have the courage to answer that question. Between the fifth and sixth she chastised herself for cowardice. And on the eighth ring she jumped up and snatched the receiver with the fervor of a drowning victim grabbing a life ring.

"Hello?"

"Hi, it's Derrick."

"I hope you're not going to start again," Cassie said abruptly. She was not in the mood for lectures, particularly about her personal life.

"I'm not starting anything. Steve called—he and Lisa are on the way to the hospital."

"*What?*" Cassie shrieked with delight. "How far apart are the contractions? Is she all right? Did her water break?" She fired the questions without allowing him time to answer.

"I don't know," her brother said with disgust when he could get a word in edgewise. "Hell, you don't think I'd ask about things like that, do you?"

"Too squeamish, huh?"

"It's nothing like—"

"You macho men can't deal with the practical aspect of childbirth," Cassie concluded smugly, aware of how her end of the conversation was also making Jake squirm. "I'll bet you'd pass out at a Lamaze class, much less survive the delivery room."

"Hell and damnation," Derrick snapped. His curse was echoed by Jake.

"Go drown your panic, brother dear," she advised. "If there's any justice in the world, a woman like Lisa is going to catch you by surprise, and then it'll be *you* rushing your wife to the delivery room." His reply was succinct and to the point. Cassie laughed and said she'd meet him at the hospital. Putting the phone down, she spun around several times with excitement.

Jake gulped, watching. She was innocently erotic. Her body was still flushed from his touch, and her hair flew about her face in a shimmer of tangled silk. She would have that look of joy the day she learned she was pregnant, only he wouldn't be here to see it.

Damn. His hands tightened around the bedding. He'd better get back to the city before he did something stupid, like agree to get Cassie pregnant...or ask her to marry him. *That* would be a really dumb move.

"Did you hear?" Cassie flung herself at Jake and kissed him resoundingly. "My sister-in-law is having her baby. I have to get dressed and get to the hospital. I can't believe it."

Before he could catch her close, she had whirled away again, first to the armoire holding her varied collection of sweaters and skirts, and then to the matching chest of drawers. Jake sat up against the brass headboard; if he couldn't touch, at least he could watch. Through his brief acquaintance with Cassie, he'd learned that while most of her clothes were sweetly old-fashioned, her undergarments were something to behold . . . sexy scraps of lace and silk, designed to blow a man's mind.

All at once he laughed, a low and husky sound from his throat. Cassie looked up, startled. "What's wrong?"

Jake put his hands behind his head and shrugged. "Not a damned thing."

"Sure."

The late-afternoon light sparkled through the window, highlighting the curves and shadows of her body. Jake shifted uncomfortably.

"Okay, it's your clothing," he murmured. "On the outside you wear a demure armor, telling men to keep a chivalrous distance. But underneath—" he grinned slowly "—underneath you're Delilah in lace."

Faint flags of pink appeared on Cassie's cheeks. "Delilah in lace," she scoffed. "That's crazy."

"Face it, sweetheart. You're covering a Ferrari with a brown paper sack."

"Brown paper sack or not, *you* haven't kept a chivalrous distance."

"No," he agreed. "But I'm a throwback. My genes originated before the age of chivalry. I'm more the *'ugh, me man, you woman,'* sort of guy."

"You can say that again," she mumbled, searching in a drawer. She pulled out a matching bra and garter belt.

"So, where do you get such racy underwear? It can't be in Sandpiper Cove." Jake reached down and found the satin ribbon he'd dropped earlier. He ran it between his thumb and forefinger. It was a poor substitute for Cassie's silky skin.

"My underwear isn't racy."

His eyebrows raised.

Belatedly Cassie held a sweater in front of her, trying to recover her modesty. "If you must know, I get it in Portland. There's a store near my gynecologist's office. You know...the one who's going to—"

"I know," he barked.

Exasperated, Cassie tried to put her bra on without revealing more skin than necessary. Jake just gave her a "bad boy" look and refused to turn away. Finally she dropped the sweater and yanked the bra in place. After all, what difference did it make? He'd seen her all but nude—it was too late for modesty. She'd almost succeeded in connecting the hooks when the phone rang again. She grabbed the receiver and sat on the bed. "Hello."

"Hi, it's me," said a slightly breathless voice.

"Lisa! What are you doing calling? Are you checked in? Was it false labor?" Cassie heard a chuckle from Jake as he brushed her searching fingers aside and fastened the bra himself, though not before depositing several kisses in the sensitive area between her shoulder blades.

"Easy," he whispered. "Let her talk."

Cassie settled against his chest, the telephone clutched to her ear. The sensation of Jake's jeans rubbing against her bare legs sent a pleasant shiver down her spine.

"I'm fine and it isn't false labor," Lisa said calmly. "Steve was so frantic he wouldn't wait. Derrick came by as we were leaving, so I asked him to call—it'll be hours before the baby comes."

"Is there anything you need? I'll be there in a few minutes."

"Great. Bring—" A soft gasp came across the line, and then the faint sound of rhythmic panting. Cassie tensed, almost as though it were her body going through the contraction. Jake rubbed her arms and stomach in a soothing motion. Almost a minute later Lisa sighed. "Sorry, that one took me by surprise."

"Are you okay?"

"Fine. You sound as bad as Steve."

"Sorry," Cassie said meekly. "This is new to me, too. What do you want me to bring?"

"How about Jake O'Connor?" her sister-in-law suggested with a light laugh. "He'll help break up the tension—give my husband something else to worry about."

"I doubt if the hospital allows brawling."

Jake took the phone from Cassie's hand. "Lisa? Hi, I'm Jake," he said. "Don't let this crazy woman worry you. I won't hurt him ... much." He allowed just enough drollery to his tone to make her laugh again, and for an instant he wished that he was really part of the family; that he really had a place in the unfolding drama.

They said goodbye, Cassie again promising she'd be there soon. Jake frowned, because it was the second time she'd spoken in the singular. Nor had she invited him to join her, despite Lisa's invitation.

"I'm going, too," he said just a tad belligerently.

"Oh." She smiled and shook her head at him. "That's a nice idea, but not necessary."

"You don't want me to come?"

She seemed at a loss for words. "Well...it's...it's a family thing. You'd be uncomfortable and you know how my brothers are."

"You mean you'd be uncomfortable having me there."

"No, it's not that. Oh, for heaven's sake, you don't really want to wait while Lisa has the baby, and then coo at him or her through the nursery window."

He gave her a dirty look. "I may be a confirmed bachelor, but that doesn't mean I hate babies or the women who have them."

Cassie pulled a stocking over her leg and fastened it to her garter belt. "You want to come so you can get into another testosterone shoving match with my brothers. No, thanks."

"My," he said mockingly, "is that the feminist talking? You sound like a card-carrying man-hater."

"Jake, please. This is very special to me, and I don't want Lisa upset, either."

Some of the excited joy faded from her face, leaving her uncertain and vulnerable. Jake wanted to kick himself. Why couldn't he leave it alone? Why did he have to keep pushing? "Cassie, I just want to be there. Not to fight with Derrick or Steve, just to be there. With you. I love the way you light up. Is that wrong?"

Biting her lip, Cassie pulled a brush through her hair. To be perfectly honest, she wanted him to come; she just dreaded having to spend her time refereeing between the three men. Yet surely they'd be on their best behavior, nobody would want to ruin the day for Lisa...or Steve, for that matter.

"You promise no fighting?"

"On my honor."

"None of that puffed-out-chest stuff or snide remarks?"

"I swear."

She looked at him speculatively, a faint smile tugging at the corners of her mouth. "No groping?"

"Not where they can see," he agreed. Suddenly they both grinned.

"I guess you can come, then."

"Phew." Jake pretended to wipe his brow of sweat. "You're a hard sell. I'd hate to be a vacuum-cleaner salesman in your neighborhood."

"Idiot."

They met Virgie on their way out to the car. In the mysterious manner of small towns, she'd already learned that Lisa was having her baby. As Cassie's self-appointed substitute mother—and therefore holding a remote claim to being grandmother to the arriving infant—she was also headed for the hospital. Jake sighed to the inevitable and suggested they drive together.

"Did Cassie make you promise to behave?" Virgie asked suspiciously before agreeing.

"Yes."

"Smart girl."

When they arrived at the hospital waiting room, Derrick was staring glassy eyed at a fetal-development chart. There was a nasty green pallor on his face, and a muscle in his throat worked violently. With a struggle Cassie kept from laughing.

A second later Steve came flying down the hall shouting for the doctor. He stormed by his sister without seeing her. If the expression on Derrick's face was squeamish, the father-to-be's could only be called terror. He grabbed the first nurse he found.

"She's *hurting*," he cried. "Where's the doctor? Oh, God."

Curving his arm around Cassie's waist, Jake whispered, "I think you'd better check on Lisa. I'll pull him down from the rafters."

To Cassie's surprise, Jake seemed calm and ready to take charge—something they desperately needed. He gave her a little shove, and she walked in the direction from which Steve had come, counting the room numbers as she went. When she found the right one, she walked in as Lisa was attempting to get out of the bed.

"What do you think you're doing?" she scolded.

Lisa blew a damp tendril of hair from her forehead. "My water broke with this huge contraction, and Steve got hysterical. I've changed my gown, but the sheets need to be fixed, too."

"Sit down," Cassie said firmly. Since there was a fresh supply of linen stacked on a nearby cart, Cassie didn't wait for the nurse; she simply stripped the mattress and made up the bed.

Awkwardly Lisa crawled back under the blankets. "Thanks," she sighed. "They've been awfully busy with an emergency. I hate to call for help, and it's making Steve crazy."

"Has the doctor checked you?"

"Yes...between patients. She said I'm coming along fine."

Cassie held Lisa's hand, relieved to see the tension ease from her sister-in-law's face. In less than a year, with luck, she would be giving birth herself. The prospect was both exhilarating and frightening.

"You...uh...might be interested to know that Jake took charge out there," she murmured.

"Oh? I wonder how the Cavannaugh brothers are taking it?"

"Just fine." Both women looked in the direction of the voice and saw a subdued Steve standing in the doorway. "He said I should calm down and stop overreacting. He's right," Steve admitted grudgingly. "Sorry, babe."

Cassie and Lisa glanced at each other, their heads shaking. And men thought women were unpredictable.

"I'll be outside," Cassie said, edging toward the door. "Sit down and hold your wife's hand," she ordered her brother.

Quite meekly he did just that.

The next few hours were a happy blur of waiting. Cassie could hardly sit still. She bounced up and down the corridors, in and out of Lisa's room, and spent a substantial amount of her time standing in front of the nursery window, watching the newborns. It didn't matter that her niece or nephew hadn't yet arrived; she thought all the babies were adorable.

Perhaps the funniest moment of the day was when Derrick realized the doctor was a woman. To him, doctors were supposed to be *men,* and no argument about it. He glared at the petite M.D. as if she'd broken the law, and she glared right back. Dr. Lane Carson was an import from the eastern seaboard and she didn't put up with any nonsense.

"He might be furious, but he checked her ring finger," Jake whispered in Cassie's ear. "I think one of the mighty have fallen."

"Derrick?" she scoffed. "Not much chance of that. He's almost as impervious to matrimony as you are. I thought he'd have heart failure when Steve got married. Though he's since admitted that Lisa is, and I quote, 'one hell of a woman.'"

"That's original."

"He's no poet," she acknowledged cheerfully, yet she was contemplating Jake's theory. Maybe Derrick would leave her alone if he got married. It was a selfish thought. She wanted her brother to be happy. So why couldn't he be happy with a wife and stop trying to manage his sister's life? The feisty brunette might be the answer to Cassie's prayers.

Restless again, she veered back toward the nursery. The nurse had said Lisa's contractions were only a few minutes apart, and the baby would be coming any time. It was crazy to start feeling so wistful and envious. She didn't begrudge their joy, far from it, so why did she feel so out of sorts and jittery?

Because of Jake. He hadn't changed her mind about having a baby, but he'd focused the pain of her compromise. Spreading her fingers, Cassie placed both palms on the glass, staring intently at the red-faced, squirming infants. They were beautiful. Every one of them. Perfect.

At the end of the hall Jake shoved his hands in his pockets and watched Cassie. He could have felt her yearning a mile away.

"It's that miserable biological-clock stuff," Derrick muttered from behind. "Look at her. She's practically drooling."

"Nothing is that simple," Jake said, trying to control his anger. He didn't like Cassie's decision, but he knew better than to belittle her choice or to dismiss it as some kind of hormonal urge. And like it or not, she'd make a damned good mother. He motioned Derrick into the waiting room. "She can do what she wants—she's an adult."

"I know, but that doesn't make it easier. Hellfire, she can do the damnedest things." Derrick shook his head. "Drives us crazy."

"Tell me about it."

They shared a commiserating groan. Jake thought about confiding how he'd found Cassie doing her high-wire act on the framework of the deck, then decided Derrick would just come unglued again. For the moment he felt a warm kinship with her brother. He supposed Cassie would wrinkle her nose and call it "male bonding."

"Um…" Jake hesitated. "I know this isn't the right time or place, but I've been wondering about Cassie…I mean…about when your parents were killed. It must have been terrible for her."

Derrick stared at him. "If you want to know something about my sister, then ask her. Don't come to us for the answers. When you go back to Seattle, we'll be the ones picking up the pieces."

Jake scowled. "You're Cassie's family, but you don't know anything about her. She *won't* be falling apart, and there won't be any pieces to pick up. She's stronger than you think."

"Yeah, right."

"I have more honest respect for her than you'll ever have," Jake said heatedly. "You treat her like a mindless fool."

"Really?" A queer smiled twisted Derrick's mouth. "You have it wrong. Cazz is…different. We know she can do anything she sets her mind to."

Different. Jake's mother had said the same thing. "If she's so capable, why do you want to wrap her in cotton wool?"

Derrick made a helpless gesture. "I don't know how to explain. It's like she doesn't belong anywhere, not here, maybe nowhere. It drove us crazy when she joined the Peace Corps."

Jake brushed his forehead with his hand. "Cassie was in the Peace Corps?"

"Yeah, for four years. I tried to get in, too, but they wouldn't assign me to her location."

Once again Jake's perception of Cassie took a dramatic spin before settling into a new shape. Peace Corps volunteers worked in poverty-stricken and often hazardous places.

Derrick didn't seem to notice his reaction. "At least in Sandpiper Cove we can protect Cassie," he said.

Shaking his head, Jake tried to remember the here and now and not think about the dangers Cassie had already survived. "Your heavy-handed protection is like using a bulldozer to weed a flower bed." He regarded the other man thoughtfully. In other circumstances he would have liked the eldest Cavannaugh. "You're driving her away...can't you see that?"

"All I see is some guy putting the moves on her even though he doesn't plan on sticking around."

"She knows how I feel."

"Oh? And is that supposed to make it easier when you leave?"

"She doesn't love me. She won't fall apart." *No*, Jake thought. *She'll probably hold up better than I will.*

The sound of a throat clearing caught their attention, and they looked toward the source. Lisa's doctor was standing at the door.

"You have a healthy nephew, Mr. Cavannaugh," she said.

"Lisa—"

"Is fine," the small brunette affirmed. "So is your brother...now that he's conscious."

"Damnation. You mean he fainted?" Derrick asked, disgusted.

The doctor permitted herself a smile. "Actually he knocked himself out on the door of the delivery room. I haven't seen a new father so excited since I was an intern."

"Fool," Derrick mumbled, obviously embarrassed by his sibling's lack of restraint.

Lane Carson's smile widened as she enjoyed his discomfort. "I thought it was charming."

Jake thought it was a good time to make his escape. He should have been with Cassie. Now he'd missed seeing her expression when she heard the news.

"Uh . . . wait a minute, O'Connor." Derrick stopped him at the door. "You asked about our folks' death. I don't know what you're trying to figure out, but don't make the mistake of thinking Cazz hasn't come to terms with what happened."

"How would you know?"

Derrick Cavannaugh's face was grave, despite the happy events of the day. "Better than you think, O'Connor. Much better."

Doubts circled in Jake's mind as he hunted for Cassie. The way it looked to him, nobody seemed to understand her—himself included. Each time he thought he'd found a piece of the puzzle, he got more confused.

Where was she?

All at once Cassie dashed down the corridor and flung her arms around his neck. "Jake! Have you seen the baby?" she exclaimed. She pressed excited kisses all over his face. "He's incredible."

"I haven't seen him. I was looking for you."

"Well, come on."

Grabbing his arm, she tugged him into Lisa's hospital room. It was filled with people. Lisa, her face flushed and tired, beamed as she held a small bundle. Steve, holding an ice pack against his head, grinned wider than a baboon. Virgie preened as though she'd done the deed herself. And Doctor Carson and Derrick had gritted teeth for one another and huge smiles for everyone else.

"Would you like to hold him?" Lisa held out the precious bundle to her sister-in-law.

Cassie held her breath as she took the newborn. Christopher Stephen Cavannaugh made a small noise, his lips puckering a moment before smoothing. At six pounds twelve ounces, he was the most precious baby in the world. "Oh, Lisa," she whispered. "He's so beautiful."

"Next time it'll be you," Lisa promised. The men in the room shuffled their feet. The women ignored their discomfort.

After a few minutes the doctor suggested they let mother and child get some rest. Cassie reluctantly put Christopher in his bassinet and rolled it closer to the bed. "I'll see you later." She kissed Lisa on the cheek. "Take care of my nephew."

"I will. Take care of Steve."

"I'm not going anywhere," Steve protested. He pulled a chair over next to Lisa. "Go to sleep, darling," he murmured. Both husband and wife were dozing by the time everyone had tiptoed from the room.

Jake linked hands with Cassie as they walked through the cold night air in the parking lot. He wanted to kiss her—not for any special reason, but just because she was smiling and happier than he'd ever seen her.

His mother made a pretense of a wide yawn as they pulled into the driveway back at the house. "Boy, what a night," she said. "I'm exhausted. I'll see you in the morning."

There was a short silence when she left. "Let's take a walk down by the water," Jake suggested.

After tossing her shoes on the deck, Cassie followed him down the path. He dropped an arm across her shoulders, and they wandered along the wet sand, just above the reach of the waves. After a while they sat down, Cassie between Jake's legs, with his arms about her for warmth.

Except for the sound of the breakers, the beach was quiet and empty. Cassie closed her eyes and imagined they were the only people around for hundreds of miles. It was a pleasant thought. She rubbed the back of her head against Jake's shoulder, and he shifted, cuddling her closer.

He nuzzled a kiss on her ear. "I think another storm is coming."

"Yes," she whispered. "Today it was all golden light and shimmering water. Tomorrow we'll have rain. The ocean is like that...unpredictable...always beautiful," she murmured in a voice that blended with the rise and fall of the waves.

"It's already tomorrow," Jake murmured.

"The north Pacific Coast is dangerous, especially in winter. There are lots of shipwrecks, even now with our fancy technology," Cassie continued dreamily. "In the 1800s a woman in Washington saved the lives of three men when their ship foundered on the beach in a storm. It was freezing cold and dangerous, but she risked herself to go into the water and pull them out."

"That must have taken a lot of courage."

"It was at Gray's Harbor. She was awarded a medal by the British government."

"That's nice," he breathed.

He didn't know if her story was idle wandering or if there was a deeper purpose to the telling. No one had been there to save her parents when they drowned. Did she feel responsible? Did she wonder what she could have done—a small child—to save them?

Jake focused on the dark blur of the horizon, where no defining line between the sea and sky could be detected. He wanted to ask his questions, yet he couldn't. He couldn't spoil the pleasure of holding her close and feeling so peaceful.

Instead, he stroked his cheek against Cassie's hair. He loved her hair, the scent and silky texture. If he lived to be a hundred, he'd never forget how it felt sliding across his skin, cool and hot at the same time.

Closing his eyes, Jake swore to himself.

He wanted Cassie with a special kind of agony. But it was too late. Years too late. And all the wishes and dreams in the world weren't going to change anything.

Chapter Nine

"Cassie?" Jake called as he knocked.

There was no answer. He stepped inside and glanced around. The cottage was completely silent, the only sound coming from the early morning rain on the roof.

In the two days since the baby had been born, he hadn't gotten more than a glimpse of Cassie, though he'd worked hard repairing the deck. Jake grinned as he glanced out the back window. At long last the thing was completely rebuilt. No need for Cassie to risk her neck out there, even to get his attention.

No sirree!

He'd learned his lesson. If Cassie wanted his attention, all she had to do was ask.

What about when you're in Seattle?

She can call, can't she?

Jake ignored the argumentative voice in his head. He was getting good at ignoring it, no matter how persistent the voice got. The grim reality was that Cassie wouldn't call, because she didn't need him. She didn't even need him to get pregnant; she could do that in a doctor's office.

"Damn," he mumbled. He turned and took the stairs two at a time. He wanted to hold her, to forget the dissident forces battling in his brain.

"Cassie?"

The second floor was as empty as the first. His stomach felt uneasy as he looked out on a dark, whitecapped sea, barely distinguishable from the sky.

No. She wouldn't have gone down there again.

His gaze swept the beach for an endless minute before he noticed Cassie, kneeling on the bluff, her face lifted to the sky. Relief made him sag against the casement. She was a safe distance away from the edge, swaying with gusts of wind and blending with the storm in a gray-blue sweater and jeans.

Anyone else would have looked cold and miserable crouching there, but Cassie looked as if she were part of the wind, a siren communing with Poseidon and the spirit of the earth.

"Ah . . . Cassie," he breathed.

How could any man hope to hold a woman like that? How could he be content, knowing there was a part of her he'd never be able to reach . . . or even touch. Jake shivered, though the room was warm. For several minutes he paced the room before finally sinking onto the bed.

The blankets and sheets were wildly tossed, as if she'd had a difficult time sleeping. But why? She was so happy about her new nephew. For the past two days she'd bubbled with joy and enthusiasm, reminding him of a kite dancing on the end of a string.

Jake put one pillow behind his back and held a second against his chest. He wasn't leaving, no matter how long it took...not until Cassie came back inside. If the two of them had anything in common, it was their stubbornness.

Don't stir things up. She's been through enough—what about the man who hurt her before?

"Shut up," Jake muttered. He didn't *know* she had been hurt by another man; he'd just assumed it. And she hadn't denied the assumption.

You can't stick around. You can't keep upsetting everyone. What about your bachelorhood?

"It's okay," he assured his argumentative inner voice. "Cassie knows the score." Jake buried his face in the pillow. *Mmm,* it smelled like hyacinths and Cassie's own unique, feminine fragrance. Besides, he wasn't chasing after her this time; he was staying put and letting her come to him. Surely it wouldn't take very long.

Half an hour later he was still waiting. *She just needs some time for herself,* he reasoned. Yet it worried him the way Cassie was mesmerized by the ocean. He could explain it with psychological reasoning—her parents' death, the effect of almost drowning herself—yet it didn't help. No matter what the reason, she had to let go of the terrible memories.

His mouth tightened cynically. "Right, O'Connor, like you've let go of your memories. You're a fine one to preach." Jake kicked the mattress with a restless foot.

Damn it, Cassie, come back inside.

A full hour later Jake heard the downstairs door open and close. Arranging the pillow once more behind his back, he sat up and waited. When Cassie saw him, she took a quick, startled breath.

"Jake, what are you doing here?"

"Waiting."

"For...what?" She lifted her shoulders, then shivered uncontrollably. In an instant Jake was off the bed and by her side.

"Let me help."

"I'm all r-right," she stuttered.

"Sure, if pneumonia is all right."

"I'm not...I don't get sick."

"Not ever?"

"No colds, f-flu, nothing," she said through teeth that chattered with each cold shudder.

"Damned good thing the way you abuse yourself," he snapped. "But there's always a first time. Come on." He took her to the bathroom and stripped the wet clothes, running a continuous monologue under his breath about the insanity of someone deliberately courting a typhoon.

"I'm all right," she protested, pushing his hands away and trying to cover herself.

"No, you're not," he said, lifting her into the old-fashioned bathtub and turning on the hot water. Cassie curled up and hugged her knees.

"Why didn't you come in earlier?" Jake demanded. "You're practically frozen."

"I don't feel the cold, not when I'm out there."

He sighed and for a moment rested his forehead against the palm of his hand. *Of course not.*

"Why, Cassie? Why do you go out like that? It scares the hell out of me," he said harshly.

"You don't need to worry."

"Really? That's bloody nice of you."

Cassie bit her lip and hugged her legs tighter. "Virgie must be wondering where you are," she said in a small voice.

"I'm sure my mother knows I'm here and is delighted. She's probably planning the wedding right now. Or maybe buying baby furniture," he said, the words tinged with irony.

Closing her eyes, Cassie put her head against her knees and rocked, feeling warmth return in painful twinges. "It's not . . . I'm sure she knows better."

Jake wanted to kick himself. There was no need to defend himself against Cassie's machinations, only against the shimmering lure of her sensuality. "I'm sorry," he murmured. He slid his finger under her chin and lifted. Her eyes were enormous in her white face. Beautiful and hurt. "I'm really sorry."

"So am I."

"It's not your fault." He stroked wet tendrils of hair from her forehead, trying to resist the enticement of her sleek, wet skin. "It's me. I'd give anything to be the right kind of man for you. But I can't be."

For an instant anger simmered in the blue-gray depths of her eyes, erasing the hurt. Then that, too, faded. "I haven't asked you to be anything," she said sadly. "Maybe that's the problem."

No, the problem is that you don't really need me. Appalled because he'd almost spoken the words aloud, Jake clenched the hand resting on his thigh. He was being perversely unreasonable, the result of a decade of distrusting women. No matter what Cassie had wanted or said, he would have found a way to turn it against her. Now, because she didn't want anything from him, he was upset about that.

Forcing himself to breathe calmly, Jake settled on the floor next to the bathtub. It effectively concealed the lower half of his anatomy. *One... two... three,* he counted silently, compelling his unruly body and emotions to behave.

At the door of the bathroom, a small, furry face appeared. "Meroowwit," the cat complained.

Cassie extended her fingers, keeping one arm protectively around her bent legs. "Come here, Shadow," she coaxed.

The feline stepped daintily across the entrance, then stood with one paw poised in the air. His whiskers twitched in plaintive displeasure at the puddles streaking the floor. "Mrrrow," he complained again.

If Jake hadn't felt so miserable, he would have laughed. The once-half-drowned cat was behaving like a prima donna.

"Shadow, it's all right."

Skirting both the puddles and Jake, Shadow leapt and teetered on the rounded edge of the tub. Then, in a feat worthy of a high-wire artist, he walked around and wedged himself against the adjacent wall. As he waved his tail in the air, a booming purr rippled out of his throat.

Cassie stroked her finger across one whiskered cheek. "Good boy," she whispered.

A pink tongue emerged from Shadow's face, and he licked the drops of water on Cassie's forehead. Delicately. Adoringly. A vibrating mass of pleasure.

Jake groaned.

Startled, the cat recoiled and spit at him.

"What's wrong?" Cassie asked, turning her head.

"That damned cat."

The faint flushing of Cassie's skin might have been from the hot water, but Jake was willing to bet she was embarrassed. His opinion was confirmed when she wiggled into a tighter ball.

It didn't help.

The most intimate parts of her body were hidden, but the parts that showed were equally alluring—from the ripe swell of her breasts above her closely pressed legs to the elegant curve of her waist, descending into the water.

"I'm fine now," Cassie said. "You can leave me alone."

"Mmm, I'd better stay. You're still shivering."

"Rat," she breathed.

He pretended not to hear.

"I'm not shivering," she said louder. "Please leave so I can wash my hair."

"I'll help." He received a fulminating glare. Lazily Jake reached for the shampoo and squirted a fair amount into his palm. "Just relax. I love playing with a woman's hair," he said with a grin. "Especially long hair. It's very sexy." With his other hand he scooped water over Cassie's head, spraying drops in every direction. Shadow spit at him and quickly scrambled out of range.

As he massaged the fragrant soap into Cassie's hair, Jake became aware she was trembling again. He reached for the hot-water tap, but the sound of choked laughter stopped him.

"Hey, what's so funny?" he demanded.

Cassie looked up, swiping bubbles from her forehead. "You are. There's nothing sexy about a blue woman with 'rat tails' on her head."

"You aren't blue," Jake denied. And he couldn't imagine anyone calling Cassie's luxuriant mass of hair "rat tails."

She made a face. "I guess not. Now I'm an unattractive red." Gloomily she surveyed her arms. She had relaxed her hold around her legs, enough for Jake to glimpse the deep rose aureoles around her nipples.

"No, you're not. You're a mermaid," he said desperately. On a nearby cabinet a neat stack of washcloths caught his attention. He grabbed one and handed it to her. "Here, cover your eyes and lean forward. I'm going to rinse." He barely gave her enough time to make a muffled protest before scooping more water over her head.

Another peal of laughter came from under the washcloth.

Jake blinked, focusing on his hands. Wet, Cassie's hair was darker—a rich cinnamon, shot with gold and red. He could play with it forever and never tire of the heavy, brightly layered texture.

"Damn," he mumbled.

"Damn what?" Cassie asked, still cheerful. "My hair? Get a pair of scissors and cut it off. I can't wash it properly without a shower anyway."

"You can't cut it off. I told you...it's sexy," Jake growled. "In a boy's fantasy of knightly valor and beautiful maidens, the girl always has long hair."

"But you don't have those fantasies...not any longer," she reminded him quietly, her face still hidden.

Jake's fingers stilled for a moment. Nothing could make him an idealistic boy again. In a child's imagination the men were always brave, and the women beautiful and steadfast. Infidelity and divorce were the brutal reality. He'd learned his lesson the hard way.

But not Cassie. She could never be a cheat, not with her body and not with her emotions.

"I ... uh ... don't suppose you'd consider lying back and rinsing properly," he suggested gruffly.

"What do you think?"

"I think you're stubborn enough to leave the soap in it."

"There's a bucket in the corner," she said promptly. "Use that to rinse ... if you won't go away."

"I won't." Jake took the container and ladled bucket after bucket of water over her head.

"Thanks...I think," she said, pushing the hair from her face when he finished. The long locks trailed over her shoulders, concealing the curves of her breasts.

"You're welcome." He hesitated. It wasn't fair to ask her questions, not when she was trapped. "Cassie, what's wrong? You've been so happy about the new baby. It doesn't make sense."

"I ... they brought him home last night," she murmured. "We had a party, with balloons and banners. He slept so quietly in the middle of the excitement, like a little angel. You should have seen Steve and Lisa ... they were so happy. Then Derrick got there. He saw me holding Christopher and immediately started preaching that I didn't need a baby of my own when I had a nephew."

Jake took her hand, tracing the slender lines. "Cassie...have you thought about...I mean, that he might be right? It's hard having a child alone."

"So I'm told."

"I know it's none of my concern, but—"

"You're right—it isn't your concern." She pulled her hand free. Her face, usually so warm and expressive, was bleak. "You don't have any voice in my life. That's the way you want it, remember?"

Jake had wanted a lot of things, and none of them seemed to be coming right. He wished he was noble enough to support her decision, but it galled him to think of another man's child growing in her body.

It should be mine.

No.

The counterpoints of rationality and emotion fought with each other, neither winning. But Cassie wasn't a point or argument; she was a tender, giving woman who wanted a child.

Which left them on different sides of a very wide ocean.

"I'm sorry," he said softly. "I keep saying the wrong thing... and this time I shouldn't have said anything."

"Then why did you?"

"Because I'm a jerk."

A faint smile trembled on her lips. "Really?"

"Yeah, really. You should have nailed me the minute I opened my stupid mouth."

"I can't nail all the jerks in my life," Cassie said, her smile becoming wider.

"Speaking of which... do you remember that first night on the beach?" Jake asked. Looking surprised, she nodded. "I assumed you'd been hurt by someone... because of how you acted and what you said about me lowering my standards because no one else was available."

She made a quick, almost involuntary movement, and he wasn't sure if it was from what he'd said or if her muscles were still reacting from the cold.

"Who was it?" Jake prompted.

Spreading her fingers, Cassie stared at the redness of her skin. "Nobody," she muttered. When he didn't say anything, she glanced at him from the corner of her eye, then sighed. "Some guy at college. I was a freshman, he was a junior."

"Were you in love with him?"

She shrugged. "No, but for a while I thought I might be. It turned out I was a filler, between more 'interesting' girlfriends. He came from a wealthy background, but his parents had cut his allowance. He figured he wouldn't need to spend as much money on me."

"Idiot," Jake said succinctly.

"In more ways than you think," Cassie said. She rested her head on her knees and yawned. "The last I heard he'd been divorced several times."

"You don't sound too upset about it." Jake stroked the length of Cassie's back. She moaned with pleasure.

"I'm not...at least not anymore."

"No regrets?"

"Only that I was stupid enough to throw my virginity away on him. At least I could have slept with someone who would have valued it instead of thinking it was funny."

Jake's hand tightened into a fist. In his youth he'd been as insensitive as the guy who'd hurt Cassie. He wouldn't have valued her virginity, not the way she deserved. "How can you still believe in love," he asked, his voice harsh, "after that? I don't understand."

"I don't know." Cassie rubbed her face. "Maybe if I'd really been in love with him it would have hurt more, but I wasn't. I think my pride and self-esteem were more damaged than my heart, and I couldn't let someone so worthless destroy me...could I?"

Standing, Jake lifted Cassie from the bathtub and wrapped her in a fluffy towel. She nestled against his chest with all the sleepy trust of a child, and something between wonder and pain twisted in his throat.

"You're beautiful," he said, his tone rough. "Beautiful and sexy and—" He stopped short when she tipped her head and gave him a drowsy smile.

"You don't have to bolster my confidence," she murmured.

"I'm just telling the truth."

"Sometimes the truth is dangerous."

"Don't I know it," Jake said, rueful. With Cassie pressed against him he had no more hope of concealing his desire than he had of flying around Neptune. "Come on, mermaid." He lifted her in his arms and carried her to the bed. "You need some sleep."

"But it's morning."

"Then you won't need a bedtime story." Quickly, efficiently Jake unrolled the towel and tucked her under the sheets in one swift motion. Something close to disappointment flashed across Cassie's face.

"I need to dry my hair," she objected.

He sighed, resigned. He wasn't going to get out of the cottage unscathed. "I'll get the dryer."

When he returned, Cassie was sitting up, a sheet wrapped toga style around her body. She held out her hand, but he shook his head. "Move over," he ordered.

Cassie shimmied to the center of the bed with a movement just short of lethal to a man's self-control. He plugged the hair dryer into the wall and sat behind her. For long minutes he ran the brush through her hair, directing the hot air to dry it evenly. Slowly the damp strands became a sleek, glistening fountain of gold, curling around his hands and arms.

In the quiet of the room after he turned the dryer off, he could hear her breathing unnaturally fast. Jake curled his fingers into the glossy strands and pulled her against his chest. "Better?" His voice was thick with silent need.

"Better."

He could swear the same need was tearing Cassie apart.

"I'd better leave."

"Uh-huh."

At the door Jake stopped and looked back. "How about dinner—tomorrow night?"

"Do you think that's smart?"

"Hell, no."

"In that case... how about six o'clock?"

Chapter Ten

*P*ositive. Cassie stared at the indicator, stunned. She hadn't been keeping good track of her cycle since the beginning of Jake's visit. He'd thrown her completely off kilter, making her forget important things like charting her temperature.

The past few days had been both strange and wonderful, Jake treating her with an old-fashioned courtliness. He didn't touch; he just looked with an unveiled hunger that set her heart racing. Without ever discussing the matter, they'd come to a consensus—if they touched, the conclusion would be inevitable. So instead they talked, laughed and kept a safe distance.

And they didn't talk about the baby... the yet-to-be-conceived baby Cassie wanted more than she wanted a short-term affair with Jake.

Cassie looked at the indicator again. She'd slept late, then suddenly become wide awake, remembering her carefully laid plans. There was no doubt. According to the charts, the temperature she'd just taken and the expensive little test kit

from the doctor's office—she was ovulating. If she wanted
to get pregnant, she had to leave for Portland immediately.
If?

No, when. Now. Yesterday if possible. Nothing had
changed Cassie's mind about the baby. So what if Jake
didn't understand. He'd made things very clear about their
relationship. No babies. No marriage.

Quickly Cassie made two phone calls. One was to the
doctor in Portland handling the insemination procedure. He
said to come right in, and they would make a time available
for her. The second was to Virgie, who put up more of an
argument.

"Please," she wailed. "I'm sure Jake will change his
mind."

Sighing, Cassie shook her head, even though the woman
on the other end couldn't see the motion. "I'm not asking
him to 'change his mind.' As far as I'm concerned, having
his baby was never a possibility."

"Darn that son of mind," Virgie fumed. "He's blinder
than a bat. I want a grandchild."

"Genetics aren't everything," Cassie reminded softly.
"You can still be a grandmother to my child, and Christopher Stephen, for that matter. You know Lisa's parents are
gone, too."

Virgie cleared her throat. She sounded suspiciously as
though she was crying. "I'll be your Lamaze coach if you
like."

Cassie bit her lip, trying not to cry herself. "Sounds great.
Look, I have to get going. I'll see you this evening.
And... Virgie? Don't tell Jake. I'll explain it to him later."

Cassie tossed a change of clothes in a bag and hurried out
the door. It was better for everyone that she just do this
quietly, with the least amount of fuss.

Besides, conceiving a baby was very personal; she didn't
want it to become more public than it already had.

Jake looked at the puppy sitting in the passenger seat and
chuckled. It was a great puppy. Purebred. Healthy. Full of

energy. A perfect gift for Cassie. He'd even build a dog run next to the cottage for her. There was enough time before he went back to Seattle.

"Darn," he muttered, pulling into the driveway. Cassie's car was missing. He knew she hadn't planned on working at the senior center that morning, but she was a busy lady. Too busy. She had a full schedule, filled with everything from coaching the soccer team to volunteering at the hospital.

"Come on, pal." Jake lifted the puppy and tucked him under his arm. "For once I'll cook for her."

He opened the door of the cottage, frowning again when he realized it was unlocked. Even Cassie was usually cautious about locking her doors when she was gone. The vague sense of disquiet in Jake grew stronger when he realized she'd neither made her bed nor eaten breakfast.

He left the squirming puppy in the kitchen and hustled over to the main house. "Mom? Do you know where Cassie's gone?"

"She's...she's just out," she said quickly and turned, but not before Jake saw her red-rimmed eyes.

"Hey, what's the matter?"

"Nothing. I don't know what you're talking about." Virgie squared her shoulders and lifted her chin. "Would you like something to eat?"

"No, I want to know where Cassie is."

"Sorry, but I can't tell you."

Something in her angry, accusing expression sent a chill down his spine. "Mother, she didn't go to Portland, did she? To that doctor?" Her gaze flickered, and Jake clenched his jaw against a few blistering words. "Where? I want the address."

"I don't have the address, and I haven't any idea what you're talking about." Virgie sniffed and plopped down on the couch. "Go away and leave me alone."

Jake obliged, feeling a mixture of emotions that ranged from outraged panic to childish sulkiness. How could Cassie do something like this? For several minutes he indulged himself with a fit of temper, then he started searching the cottage. He could try to stop her, but first he had to find out where she'd gone.

Twenty minutes later he held a bill from a Portland doctor in his hand. As he was stomping out the door, the puppy let out a pitiful howl. Shadow had immediately formed a dislike for his new housemate and was sitting in front of the food bowl, hissing at the dog.

"Ah, hell." Jake grabbed the puppy and a basket and settled them in the car.

Dirt spun under the wheels as he reversed, then accelerated out to the road. Get pregnant with another man's baby, would she? He'd see about that.

Jake should have been feeling more reasonable by the time he sped into Portland two hours later, but instead he was ready to chew nails. He parked in front of the professional building and jumped out of the car. The doctor's name was on an index in the lobby, indicating his office was on the fifth floor.

The three minutes he waited for the elevator were the longest in Jake's life. The minute it took the elevator to reach the appropriate floor seemed equally long. He then stalked down the hallway, threw open the door of the office and stormed in.

"Cassie!"

Cassie groaned and tried to hide behind her magazine. He spotted her anyway.

"What do you think you're doing?"

"Having a baby," she said, trying to sound calm. One of them had to be rational, and it obviously wasn't going to be Jake.

"The devil you are."

The other women in the waiting room perked up at the diverting display. They were in various stages of pregnancy, and waiting for the doctor normally consisted of mostly boredom and discomfort.

"This isn't any of your business," she retorted.

"I'm making it my business. We have to talk."

"All *right*. I'll be back in a few minutes," she informed the receptionist. She followed Jake to the elevator and proceeded to glare at him all the way down to the ground level. "You don't own me, Jake O'Connor."

"I never said I did."

"Then why are you trying to stop me? I'll never understand men. This has nothing to do with you."

"Me? Hell, I don't understand *you*. You're trying to pressure me into a decision," he said, knowing how idiotic he sounded.

Cassie bit on her lip hard enough to draw blood. She was so mad she was shaking. "There isn't a decision to be made—there never has been. Getting me pregnant was your mother's idea, not mine. I don't expect *anything* from you."

"Can't you just wait?" he pleaded.

"You don't understand."

"That's right, I don't." Jake slouched against the hood of his car. He noticed he'd gotten a parking ticket and was tempted to rip the thing into shreds as a vent for his frustration. "Why did you ask my mother to keep it a secret?"

Shifting her feet, Cassie felt a fleeting sense of guilt. "I . . . I just thought it would be easier. Look, this is uncomfortable enough for me. I didn't want to discuss it and I certainly didn't want an argument."

"Then you knew I'd be upset."

"I knew you didn't approve. It's the same thing."

"Hell, how else should I feel? You're a single woman living in a conservative little flea speck of a town."

"Oh? So that's what bothers you. Then it would be different if I lived in Portland or Seattle? Maybe I should just move to New York, then nobody's eyebrows would raise."

The thought of Cassie in New York, or one of the other higher-crime cities in the world, made Jake's blood pressure soar. He shoved his hands in his pockets so she wouldn't see them shaking. "That isn't the answer," he muttered.

"Why not? You said Sandpiper Cove was a flea speck, and I guess it is. In a big city nobody would care what I did. Nobody would fuss or be scandalized. No one would even notice. I think getting involved and caring about your neighbors must be against big-city ordinances."

There was enough truth in Cassie's sarcasm to make Jake wince. Granted, there was an impersonal element to city life. That's what he liked about it. Still, it wasn't gossiping neighbors that really bothered him about her having a baby.

"What—" His voice cracked and he cleared his throat. "What if I offered to...you know, get you...uh..."

"Pregnant?"

"Uh...yes. I mean...it's not such a bad idea, now that I'm used to it."

"How generous," she murmured. "You're offering to get the little spinster pregnant. Shall we visit the doctor or just have a tumble in bed?"

Damnation. He should have known better than to say anything. Cassie had a sharp tongue when she was angry, and right now she was furious enough to slice strips off his hide. With a dull knife.

"I just thought—"

"You didn't think," she interrupted. "You don't care about my having a baby. The real issue is your pride."

Jake didn't know if it was pride plaguing him or plain old-fashioned selfishness. He wanted Cassie for himself, but he was too damned scared of falling in love with her to take the chance. And he didn't want to share her with anyone else— even a nameless stranger's baby.

"I just don't see why you can't wait," he repeated a little desperately. "Is it the end of the world if you wait until next month?"

"Next month, when you won't be around and won't have to deal with it. Or maybe you think I'll just change my mind if I give the matter some thought...." '

"Yes...no...I don't know. I got back to the cottage with a present for you and found you gone. How was I supposed to react?"

Cassie knew the last thing she should do was ask, but she couldn't help herself. "What present?"

"I...uh..." Jake fished his keys from his pocket and opened the door of his BMW. He leaned in, made an encouraging sound and turned around. "Here he is."

She blinked. Jake was holding a puppy, a darling puppy with a wet nose and anxious expression, who was dumped unceremoniously into her arms. "Wait—"

"He's all yours. It's a golden retriever."

"I know that." She shifted the pup and scratched his silky ears. He burrowed into her neck with a whimpering sigh. "But why a dog?"

"You said you wanted a dog, so I got you one."

"I already have Shadow."

"Now you have both. Come on, it'll be nice. Animals are fun. They're entertaining, and—"

"And you figure they're a nice substitute for a baby." She shoved the puppy back at him. "Nice try."

"That isn't what I meant. Stop putting words into my mouth."

Cassie didn't need to put words in his mouth; she'd seen it in his face. It was his way of patting her on the head like a child and offering ice cream as a consolation. No matter how much she'd wanted Jake to accept her decision, he hadn't. He hadn't even come close.

"I'm going back to the office," she said quietly. She felt more alone than ever. "I guess I was foolish to hope you'd understand, much less support me."

"Cassie, please, I—" Jake held out his hand, but she was gone. "Damn," he whispered. He hadn't consciously thought of the puppy as a substitute for a baby. Undeniably, though, the thought must have been in the back of his mind.

The small animal wriggled until he could land a wet lick on Jake's face.

"Hey, pal." Jake scratched the pup's neck. "I blew it, didn't I? Don't worry, she'll forgive you."

The question was, would Cassie ever forgive Jake?

Cassie endured the whispering and curious glances of the other patients with a red face. She almost bolted out the door when one of the women asked if she was okay and whether she needed a tissue or anything.

"No, I'm fine," she said quickly. She looked longingly at the receptionist, praying they would call her name. *Wanting* a baby wasn't the problem—having the courage to deal with the consequences was another issue.

Jake... No, she refused to think about him.

"Ms. Cavannaugh? The doctor will see you now."

Cassie felt her heart race and she willed her stubborn pulse to slow down. Ten minutes later it was churning at the speed of a locomotive, but for an entirely different reason. She stomped out of the office and down to her car. She was going to *kill* Jake. He was mincemeat. He was going to regret ever setting eyes on her.

Disregarding the speed limit, Cassie reached Sandpiper Cove in record time. "He'd better be home," she growled to herself as she careened out the coast road to the cottage. She slammed to a stop in the driveway, narrowly missing Jake's fender by two inches. In her mood she would have enjoyed denting the shiny BMW for the pleasure of seeing him react.

She leaned on the doorbell of the main house until Virgie answered. "Where is he?" she asked without preamble.

"What's wrong?"

"I want to talk to your son."

"Now, Cassie, I don't blame you for being annoyed. I didn't tell him where you'd gone, I really didn't. He just guessed."

Cassie gritted her teeth. Virgie would be delighted to learn the real reason she was upset. "I'm not annoyed at you. I'm furious with Jake. *Where is he?*"

"Er...well, he's out on your deck."

Cassie turned and marched across the compound, around the corner of the cottage and up the three steps to the deck. Sure enough, Jake was leaning on the railing and gazing at the ocean. If she hadn't been so angry, she would have felt some regret at the dejected slump to his shoulders.

To get his attention she slammed her large purse down on the ground. The heavy object made a satisfying clunk, and he twisted around, startled.

"Cassie?"

"Yes, it's me. And thanks to your interference, the doctor wouldn't do it."

"I...what do you mean? He didn't do the procedure?" It was impossible for Jake to feel happy about the news, not when he saw a flood of unshed tears in her beautiful eyes.

"He said, and I quote, that 'maybe I should get my relationships in order before I make such a momentous choice.' He suggested that your appearance at the office might mean I had a future with you and that I should give the possibility a shot," she concluded, disgusted.

"Well, I—"

"He wouldn't listen when I explained that a future with you was as improbable as pigs flying. He said I could come back in three or four months if I'm still interested."

"I'm sorry—"

"And wasn't it nice? He said he wouldn't charge me for today's visit. Big of him, wasn't it? I won't have to pay for his doing nothing."

"Can I get a word in edgewise?" Jake growled.

She shrugged and leaned against the wall of the cottage, crossing her arms over her breasts. There was nothing the man could say that would make her feel better. "Suit yourself."

"I didn't mean to mess things up," Jake said unhappily. "I'm really sorry. I reacted without thinking how it would affect you."

"That's nice."

Jake sighed, knowing Cassie had every reason to hate him. In all probability, forgiveness wasn't going to be high on her list of priorities for a long time. "I meant what I said about getting you pregnant myself. So you can still...go through with things."

"No, thanks. I told you I don't want your genes in my baby. I haven't changed my mind." Cassie grabbed her purse and stomped to the door, keys in hand.

"Cassie, be reasonable," Jake pleaded as he followed. "Mom's right—it would be the best solution for all of us."

"It isn't a solution at all. You'd be sorry the minute you started. I am *not* that desperate for a father. I could hang out at any bar and get someone just as likely."

"Don't you dare." Jake slammed the door, frightened she might actually be serious.

"Don't give me orders. You're not one of my brothers."

"Thank God for that. Besides, you don't listen to them any more than you do me."

Suddenly Cassie was sorry she'd confronted Jake, because now he wasn't going to leave without a fight and she wanted to be by herself. "Go away," she shouted.

"No."

"This is my home."

"I don't give a damn. I want you to promise you won't do anything foolish."

She scowled and shook her head. He might not be one of her brothers, but he thought he could boss her around. "I'm not promising anything."

Jake frowned heavily. "Barhopping is dangerous."

"Lots of things are dangerous," she retorted.

From the corner of her eye Cassie saw the puppy tucked into a basket by the stove. He was sound asleep. Shadow was glancing between her and the pup, tail swishing, as though to ask "what are you going to do about this upstart in my home?" He had a cat's natural arrogance and it hadn't taken him long to become possessive about the cottage. Or Cassie.

She crouched down and stroked his fur. Shadow began purring and rubbing himself along her arm.

"Cassie, talk to me."

"There isn't anything to say—except to take your dog and leave. My cat doesn't like him." As if to prove her point, Shadow spit at the puppy.

"I didn't buy him for me. Hell, he'll be protection for you and...uh...the baby." Jake was proud of the way he'd said "baby" without choking on the word. "He's from good bloodlines, with papers and everything."

"How nice. You invested in a purebred. You must have spent a bundle—I'm really impressed."

Jake was tempted to strangle the woman. Barring that, he wanted to spend about fifty hours in bed with her, making her see reason. "I didn't get him to impress you."

"No, you got him as a substitute for a baby. I'm *sooo* grateful. Please leave before I burst into sentimental tears."

"You won't go into town?"

"Right now I'm going for a walk on the beach. *Alone.*"

There was a bitter taste in Jake's mouth. "That's right, go ahead and escape. Keep running away from life. Be alone with your precious ocean."

"What?" She stared at him in shock. "I'm not running away from anything."

"No? They why do you go to the beach every time something upsets you? Why are you so entranced with storms and wind and losing yourself out there? No matter what happens, it won't bring your parents back. Storms happen—they're unpredictable."

There. He'd said it. He'd voiced his misgiving about her fascination with the sea. If she wanted to deny it, let her try.

"Is that what you think?" Cassie asked, strangely quiet. "That I have some sort of compulsion because of my parent's deaths?"

"It's . . . reasonable."

"Not really."

For several minutes Cassie was silent. She looked at Jake, not really seeing him, then automatically walked to the counter and started a pot of coffee brewing. She'd known he was uncomfortable with her walks on the shore, but she'd dismissed his reaction as unnecessary concern for her safety. The last thing she'd expected was some crazy notion about her parents.

Taking a stoneware mug from the cupboard, Cassie traced the slightly rough rim before looking up. "My mother and father were killed when the engine exploded on our boat."

A strangled sound came from Jake's throat. He threw out his hand as though to stop the explanation from coming. "Don't."

She continued, seeming not to hear him. "The water was calm, and there wasn't a cloud in the sky. The ocean didn't kill them—it could have happened anywhere."

"It's all right."

"No, it isn't." Her fingers tightened around the mug with bruising intensity. "They died because of a stupid accident. I was perched on the railing and the force of the explosion threw me overboard. My clothing was on fire, but the wa-

ter put out the flames. The cold water kept the burns from
hurting until the Coast Guard got to me.''

The cold might have controlled Cassie's physical pain, but
Jake knew nothing had dulled the horror of seeing her
mother and father die in such a way. She'd lived with that
memory for most of her life, and yet she was strong and
gentle, with a serenity that defied her darkest memories.

"They said it was a miracle I didn't die of exposure,"
Cassie murmured. "But I knew the ocean wouldn't kill me.
I've always felt connected to it, since before I can remem-
ber, so I guess you think that confirms your theory."

Jake was finished with theories and rationalizations about
Cassie. She would never fit a mold of anyone's making. A
man who loved her would need a lot of courage, because he
would have to accept her as she was and he would never
claim all of her.

Was that his real problem?

Not just distrust of love and all the pain and betrayal it
could bring, but the fear of never really having Cassie as his
own? He would have to share her with something indefin-
able. It would be like that morning, when he'd waited for
her to come in from the storm, feeling cut off as she swayed
in the wind and listened to its voices.

Maybe he was afraid of needing Cassie, because he could
never survive her loss. She wouldn't leave Sandpiper Cove,
and he couldn't stay.

"I...I don't know what to say."

"Don't say anything."

"Cassie, what are we going to do?"

She didn't answer, because there wasn't an answer.

Reaching out, Jake drew his hand down the curve of her
cheek. She was soft, so wonderfully soft, and he feared it
would be the last time he ever touched her. He'd promised
his mother he'd stay longer than he had. But it was impossible. He had to leave, had to cut his so-called vacation short

and escape. He couldn't wait around, watching Cassie, knowing they couldn't be together.

For a long moment Jake just stood there, looking, trying to impress in his memory how she looked, how she felt. "I wish things could be different," he whispered. Then he turned and left without saying goodbye.

Jake walked straight to his bedroom and pulled out his suitcases. Clothing went willy-nilly into the luggage, while Virgie stood at the door and watched.

When the last sock was stuffed inside, Jake snapped the cases shut and tried to think of something to say.

"I have to go back to Seattle. I'm sorry, I can't stay. I know we haven't spent much time together—I'm sorry about that, too," he managed. He wouldn't resort to subterfuge for an excuse. When she didn't say anything he sighed. "Mom?"

"It's all right, son." Her eyes were sad and full of understanding. "I didn't know you'd fall in love with her."

"I'm not in love with Cassie," he said quickly. Too quickly.

"No?" Virgie shrugged. "Then I guess you're not. But I still feel responsible. After all this time I should have known better than to interfere."

"It's okay. You should know what happened—she's pretty upset, but not with you. Apparently the doctor wouldn't do the insemination because of a scene I made in his office. I feel like a hypocrite. I didn't want her to have a baby, but now I feel guilty. I offered to get her pregnant instead, and she acted like it was an insult."

Virgie sat on the bed and tapped one of the suitcases with her finger. "I'm not surprised. We women can be pretty strange about some things, especially when our hearts are involved. Your father had to put up with a lot over the years."

Sitting beside her, Jake captured his mother's restless hand. "It's been a long time since he died. I know you've been lonely. I should have been here more."

"Lonely?" Virgie shook her head. "Not really. You'd be astonished by the kind of mischief I can get into...even in a little place like Sandpiper Cove."

Something in her glinting smile make Jake pause, then take a longer look. "Mom, you don't mean..."

With a laugh she squeezed his hand consolingly. "Son, I may be in my sixties, but that doesn't mean I'm dead. The fire burns just as hot—it just takes a little longer to get going."

To his eternal mortification, Jake felt himself turn red. "But Dad—"

"Your father wouldn't have wanted me to bury myself in his grave. It doesn't mean I loved him any less."

"I guess it's my day for surprises. I just never thought...I mean, this isn't much of a place. The town is so...so quiet."

Virgie laughed merrily. "Us old-timers can find a lot of trouble—even in the middle of 'nowhere,' as you call it."

The heat in Jake's face intensified. "Sorry...I know how you love it here."

"Oh, son." Her head shook. "You've never seen the potential of this little town. Besides all the good things, there's enough scandal and back-fence hopping in Sandpiper Cove to write a hundred steamy novels. Small towns don't mean dull—they just mean your neighbor knows your business as soon as you do."

"You mean there's no privacy."

"That's not the point. You once told me that Cassie wanted fairy tales and myths. That she wanted—how did you put it?—marriage and babies, and to live in a little town on the edge of nowhere...."

"That's right."

"Is it?"

"I'm sure—" His denial skidded with his thoughts. Was that what Cassie really wanted? Marriage and babies, of course, but myths and fairy tales? She hadn't been spared the heartaches in life, so she must know the difference between reality and fiction.

Virgie looked satisfied at the thoughtful expression on her son's face. "Give it some thought, Jake. Go back to Seattle if you must, only do some thinking while you're there. I know loving Cassie scares you, but how do you feel about living without her?"

Chapter Eleven

Cassie didn't go for her walk on the beach. She crawled into bed and stayed there for hours. It would have been easier if she could have cried. At least tears would have washed away the tight ache in her throat and the tension in her body.

Instead, she thought about Jake. She loved him, and the feeling was every bit as terrible and wonderful as she'd known it could be. At least she'd be able to tell her child what real love should feel like, if not how to choose the right person. There was no doubt Jake was the very last man to whom she should have given her heart.

An unhappy meow came from the foot of the bed, followed by a whimper. Cassie looked down and saw Shadow and the new puppy huddled together with anxious expressions on their furry faces. The cat extricated himself and walked up to curl into the circle of her arms. Extending a paw, he tapped her jaw and rubbed his head against her breast.

"Merowwit?"

"I know," she said, her voice a quiet murmur against the sound of the waves sweeping the shore.

The puppy sidled up her legs and settled his chin on her knee. The cat didn't flick a whisker—apparently they had reached a truce. Cassie gave a shuddering sigh. If two such different creatures could come to a compromise, why couldn't she and Jake? Yet, even as the thought formed, she dismissed it from her mind. It was too much like regret, and lifetimes were wasted on regret.

She lay there another hour, accepting the wordless comfort of her two new animal friends. Then she heard the sound of a key in the downstairs lock and the heavy tread as someone climbed the stairs. She should have been frightened, but somehow she knew it was Jake, and no threat to anything but her heart.

"I had to see you again," he whispered, standing at the door. "I'm leaving in the morning."

He was pale and exhausted, and a faint smile twisted Cassie's mouth. "You look as bad as I feel," she commented.

"You look beautiful."

There didn't seem to be an adequate response. If there was beauty in the way she looked, it could only be in Jake's thoughts and eyes. She looked like any woman who had been tearing her heart out—white-faced and miserable.

"Are you taking another job right away?" she asked.

Jake nodded. "I'm due in France in a couple of weeks."

"Sounds...nice."

"Yeah," he said but without enthusiasm. "I've been there. It's a beautiful country."

Cassie shivered, hating the awkwardness of their words. They were acting like strangers. "I've heard the French people don't care for tourists."

"Sometimes. They have a lot of national pride."

Sensing the tension, Shadow walked between the two humans and hissed at Jake. He sat on his haunches, tail swishing, daring the man to infringe on his territory. It was as though the feline sensed Jake no longer had a place in Cassie's life.

Calmly Jake grabbed both animals and hauled them unceremoniously out of the room. Finding the door closed against him, Shadow set up a raucous howling. Cassie offered a ghost of a smile.

"He doesn't like you," she murmured.

"The feeling is mutual."

"Don't you like cats?"

"Not the jealous variety." Jake nudged Cassie until she made room for him on the bed, then slid next to her under the comforter.

Her throat caught painfully. "I don't think—"

"Shh," he breathed. "Just let me hold you."

Curled on her side away from Jake, Cassie watched the ocean as the sun rose. They had lain together all night, restless at times, calm at others—but not making love and not speaking. She didn't think he'd slept any more than she had.

Scarlet-and-gold tongues of color streaked across the sky, reminding Cassie of the old seamen's proverb, "Red sky at morning, sailor take warning, red sky at night, sailor's delight." It seemed a grim omen to say goodbye beneath a red morning sky.

"I'd better go," Jake whispered.

Her eyes closed against the rush of pain. "It's a long drive to Seattle," she managed to say. He nodded, and without a another word slid from the bed.

Just as he put his hand on the door, Cassie shivered. She had to make him understand, if nothing else. "Please...wait a minute."

He turned. "Yes?"

"I...about what you said, about my parents—"

"No!" Jake made a sharp cutting motion. "I didn't have any right. I'm sorry."

"Please." Cassie held out her hand until he relented and sat beside her on the rumpled bed.

"I shouldn't have questioned you," he muttered.

"I don't mind your questions," Cassie said evenly, the truth as evident in her tone as in her words. She continued, speaking softly yet clearly. "I want you to understand. I've always felt pulled to the ocean—from before I could remember."

Jake thought of that first night when he'd lain there beside her, listening to Cassie's dreams and plans. She'd spoken of life, of a soul-burning love, and he'd become angry. He'd wanted her to dream of possibles—maybe because he was no longer capable of dreaming himself. Yet it was Cassie who knew how to compromise. It was Cassie who knew there were hard choices to be made and had the courage to make them. It was Cassie who had tried to lift his eyes from the ground to the sky. And it was Jake who had failed.

When he stayed silent, she continued, stroking her fingers across his arm. "Maybe the way my parents died does have something to do with it. Lots of children are drawn to the ocean, and I might have grown out of those feelings if things had been different. Most people do. They turn into adults with other interests, their lingering fondness satisfied by vacations in Bermuda."

"I can't imagine you in Bermuda."

"Neither can I," she said, laughing softly. "Yet who knows? A twist of fate might have changed me."

But then you wouldn't have been Cassie, was Jake's immediate thought. At least not the Cassie who fascinated and provoked him. He took her hand and traced the fine, strong lines of her fingers and palm. Fragility and strength. As always, he was amazed by the curious paradox.

She sat up and pressed against Jake for a single second. "You know...it doesn't matter why I love the ocean. It's okay for someone to care for a place, as long as it never becomes more important than people."

"Isn't it?"

"No, but I don't expect you to believe me."

"What—" Jake cleared his throat and tried again. "What do you see when you look at the sea?"

Cassie was silent for several minutes, then smiled faintly. "Mystery. Eternity. It's elemental, so close to the rhythm of life that there isn't any separation. Just . . . life."

Life. Not death, even though her parents had perished in the cold Oregon ocean.

How could that be?

Jake could think of little else as he drove the state highway into Portland, and then the interstate to Seattle. Everything about Cassie was filled with the essence of life. What kind of fool walked away from a woman like that?

Jake O'Connor, that's who, his conscience mocked. *Scared man, running away from the only real chance of happiness you've ever had.*

He struck a violent blow on the steering wheel, trying to push the thoughts away with physical pain. But they still crowded into his mind, taunting the vulnerable part of his soul Cassie had found and healed.

At his apartment Jake threw his suitcases on the couch and breathed the stale air of the closed rooms. He wasn't sure the windows opened, and if they did, whether the air outside was any better. His home . . . he'd spent little time here over the years, always moving, always taking another job in some corner of the world. It was nothing but an empty shell.

For one frenetic week Jake threw himself into activity. Work and play. Running and pretending. He exercised until he was beyond thinking, and then he still couldn't sleep. He didn't have any pictures of Cassie to remind him, but each time he closed his eyes her image was there, shining and clear. On the eighth night he sat, staring at the blank walls, and accepted that Cassie had become the only real, living part of his existence. He couldn't envision a future without her.

Jake tried to recall the bitterness that had once consumed him over his ex-wife, yet there was nothing but the irony of memory. He could go on pretending or he could go back to Sandpiper Cove.

At the end of the couch his suitcases still sat, unpacked and forgotten. Cassie would never believe he'd changed, not unless he could show her.

The following morning Jake made a series of phone calls. One was to his contacts in France. He told them he wouldn't be taking the assignment, after all. Suggestions were made about a replacement, and Jake felt only relief. He called various business acquaintances, then contacted a travel agent and planned another trip. This time—he hoped—he would need two tickets. Before leaving town, he collected brochures and descriptions of a very special place.

Each mile back to Sandpiper Cove took longer than the last, and by the time he arrived Jake's hands ached from gripping the steering wheel. At the house his mother waved, smiled and held up her fingers in a sign of victory. Jake hoped she was right. She pointed toward the shore, and he nodded.

The path down to the beach was the same, as was the sight of Cassie's walking in the distance. The breath caught in his throat, and all the possibilities of how she would react went racing through his mind. *Rage. Disappointment. Rejection.* At the last minute he almost panicked, then he strode forward.

"Still courting pneumonia, I see," he said when he was a few feet away.

Startled, Cassie whirled and lost her footing in the soft sand. Jake caught her before she fell.

"What...? Go away."

Strike one. Jake shook his head. "I'm not going anywhere."

"God," she moaned. "Don't do this to me."

"I want to start over."

"I can't, Jake," Cassie said frantically. "I can't start again." Trying to pull free, she stepped backward, only to have Jake tighten his grip. *No.* She was so very tired. She couldn't go through it again; she'd never survive.

"But there won't be an ending this time," Jake vowed, hating the pain in her face and knowing he was responsible. "I love you, Cassie."

If Jake hadn't been supporting her, Cassie would have fallen a second time. As it was, she blinked and felt the world recede and return. But...she couldn't have heard him say he loved her, could she? "You...I don't believe you."

"You'd better." He shook her shoulders. "I've done a lot of stupid things, but leaving you was one of the biggest. It's too bad if you don't love me, because I'm camping on your doorstep until you do."

"Oh, Jake." Her voice shook with emotion and suppressed tears. "You don't know what you're saying. It's crazy."

"You're wrong—it's the first sane thing I've done. I want to marry you and make babies, and I don't care if we live in Sandpiper Cove or on the moon."

"But you don't trust love. You don't understand my dreams. What kind of future could we have?"

Jake winced. Somehow he had to find the right words to make her understand how much he'd changed, not overnight, but with all the time they'd spent together. "Come on, we need to talk." Taking her arm, he led her up the beach until he found a protected space between two sand dunes. "Sit," he ordered.

Cassie obeyed because she didn't have strength in her legs to do anything else. A part of her thought she was dreaming and that Jake would disappear if her gaze faltered for even a second. Though he'd only been gone a week, he looked different, and she feasted her eyes on every plane of his face.

"My beautiful Cassie." Taking her hands, Jake pressed them between his own. "Don't you see? I finally realized that love and dreams come from the same place—the heart. And I do trust you—I would never have come back if I didn't. I wouldn't ask you to marry me."

A ragged sigh came from Jake's throat, and he realized he was holding Cassie's hands in a crushing grip. He loosened his fingers but couldn't let go completely.

"Don't send me away," he whispered. "Tell me you love me. Tell me I was right to come back. I love you more than the breath in my body. Remember what you said, about your parents being made for each other? That's the way I feel. You're the missing half of my soul. I need you."

Cassie looked down at their interlocked hands and felt him tremble. Then she looked into Jake's eyes and saw the vulnerable, naked emotion while he waited.... The answer to her every dream, every prayer and wish.

"Oh God, Jake." Cassie flung herself into his arms, scattering kisses across his face. She was laughing and crying at the same time. *He loved her*. All the worry and hurting, all the uncertainty meant nothing, not with the future spread before them like a golden sunburst.

They tumbled to the sand, Jake laughing as hard as Cassie. "Does this mean you'll marry me?"

"Yes! Whenever you want. I love you."

"Thank heavens. I won't have to camp on your doorstep."

"Would you have?"

Jake kissed Cassie's nose, then her cheeks and the softness of her forehead. Then very carefully he kissed her mouth. "For as long it took," he said softly. "Forever."

Color stained her skin. "That's nice."

"So is the honeymoon I have planned."

"Oh?" Cassie's eyebrows lifted.

He maneuvered her into a more comfortable position— one that involved pressing the length of his body down hers. "We're taking an old-fashioned riverboat ride down the

Mississippi. We'll land in New Orleans and spend a couple of weeks exploring the city and the bayou country.''

She bit her lip, looking both pleased and uncertain. "You said you didn't like the swamps. I know I said I wanted to visit the South, but we don't have to go for my sake."

"I want to see the bayous through your eyes," Jake whispered. "It tore me apart that day, thinking I'd never be there with you."

"So that's why you..." Her voice trailed off as understanding dawned.

"Acted like a moody fool?" He nodded. "I knew even then how I felt, but I was too stubborn to admit it. I'm not sure I can *feel* life in everything the way you do, but maybe I can see it—a little—with your help." Unable to resist, Jake stroked Cassie's hips, running his fingers up to her breasts and down again. He felt so free, so right lying with her.

For a long moment Cassie was silent. Then she looked at him intently. "We don't have to have a family," she said slowly. "I mean... I know how you feel about it."

Emotion squeezed Jake's chest, then released him gradually. He knew the cost of what she was offering and knew the depth of love that made her do it. He was lucky, so damned lucky, to have found Cassie. He would never make the mistake of forgetting.

"I want a family," he said firmly. "And we're living in Sandpiper Cove, so don't give me any argument." His tone was a teasing reminder of the way her brothers gave orders.

The corners of Cassie's mouth lifted with happiness. "Yes, sir," she said smartly. "Anything you say, sir."

"Intelligent lady. I've accepted a position at the university," he explained, becoming more serious. "I'll drive over and teach international politics a couple of days a week. And I have a home-security device I've been tinkering with—we may be able to market it soon."

"You've got it all planned out."

"It wasn't hard, not when I realized what really mattered to me." Jake touched Cassie's lips with his own. "Let's get married right away...I want to start working on that baby."

"We'll have to get a license, Mr. O'Connor," she said silkily, hooking her fingers in his belt and pulling him close. "And it's Saturday. We'll have to wait till Monday."

A deep laugh rumbled from Jake's chest. "Uh...what should we do until then?"

"God, that feels wonderful."

"You shouldn't have stayed out so long."

"Mmm." Jake dug his fingers into the pillow. Cassie was straddling his buttocks, giving his back a massage. And like the thoughtful wife she was...she was completely naked. The feel of her warmth against his skin was erotically distracting—and worth every aching muscle. "The kids *are* in bed, aren't they?"

Leaning down, Cassie allowed the tips of her breasts to brush Jake's spine. "They've been asleep for an hour."

His response was more like a groan.

"Poor darling," she cooed. "They wore you out. I should stop and let you sleep." Deftly he reached around and snagged her wrist. Cassie toppled to the mattress with a laugh. "I thought you were too exhausted to move," she teased.

"Never for this." Jake's fingers swept the curves of Cassie's body. She was so lovely...it never ceased to amaze him. He had watched her body change during each of her three pregnancies. He'd tried to ease her through morning sickness, held her hand and coached her breathing during childbirth. In each moment she had been more precious to him than the last, more beautiful. And though there was silver at his own temples, Cassie seemed younger with each gentle smile.

Wrapping a length of her hair in his fist, Jake bent and caught her lips in a deep kiss. "You should have come down with us," he said after a few minutes. "We missed you."

"I have to get those paintings done."

"Mmm," Jake said, frowning slightly as he pulled back to look in her face. "It's about time you had a formal gallery showing. You're so talented, I worry we're holding you back."

Her laugh was clear and happy. "Nonsense. I paint every day."

"And you have a huge demand for more—the coastal gift shops can't keep your watercolors in stock. It was pure chance when that New York art critic found one."

"I never dreamed of being a famous artist."

"But you're going to be one."

"Maybe." Cassie wasn't worried; whatever the future brought, they would deal with it. She was much more concerned about the immediate future, which involved making passionate love with her husband. Soon. He was already pressed against her—hot and urgent. "Er...Rafe called," she whispered. "While you were on the beach."

"Mmm..." he said, not really listening except to the breathless quaver of her voice. "What did he want?"

"J—just to tell us the Australian deal is ready to sign."

"That's nice." Jake's home-security device had proved remarkably popular, even in overseas markets. Fortunately he had a business partner to handle all the finicky, lengthy details. It left Jake with time for the important things...like enjoying his children and making love to his wife. "You taste good." He swirled his tongue around one of her erect nipples. "Yummy," he said, borrowing one of his four-year-old daughter's favorite words.

"Oh, you, I'm not leaking," she protested weakly. "Nick has been weaned for three months."

"Oh, yeah?" Jake played with her velvet crest another moment before pulling it into his mouth. Cassie arched against him, and he obliged by suckling strongly. They were both breathless when he released her, then blew on the pink dampness. "Very nice," he said approvingly, "I guess you aren't leaking."

"You . . ." She hit him with mock anger.

"Easy love, I'm very vulnerable."

"Sure."

Cassie smiled into Jake's warm green eyes. Each day, in a thousand ways, he showed her his love and happiness. For a while she had feared he'd regret his choice to marry and have children, but that had ended the day he held their first baby in his arms and wept tears of wonder.

Lifting her hand, she stroked the muscles in his shoulders. "Being a daddy agrees with you," she whispered.

Jake grinned widely. "Thank you. Isn't it about time we started working on another?"

Her jaw dropped. *"No."*

"But we don't have a lot more time. You know . . . the biological clock . . ."

"We have three beautiful children," Cassie said firmly. "Three is a nice number."

"So is four. Come on, honey, just one more?"

Exasperated, she shook her head. "That's what you said before Nick was born."

"Well, that worked out fine, didn't it?"

"Of course it did, but—"

Grinning, Jake angled himself above her. "One more," he coaxed. "Another girl. Think how happy my mother will be."

Cassie's eyes closed, a smile tugging at her lips. Jake was determined to win this battle. What could she do?

Besides, making babies was so much fun.

*   *   *   *   *

COMING NEXT MONTH

#1102 ALWAYS DADDY—Karen Rose Smith
Bundles of Joy—Make Believe Marriage

Jonathan Wescott thought money could buy anything. But lovely Alicia Fallon, the adoptive mother of his newfound baby daughter, couldn't be bought. And before he knew it, he was longing for the right to love not only his little girl, but also her mother!

#1103 COLTRAIN'S PROPOSAL—Diana Palmer
Make Believe Marriage

Coltrain had made some mistakes in life, but loving Louise Blakely wasn't one of them. So when Louise prepared to leave town, cajoling her into a fake engagement to help his image *seemed* like a good idea. But now Coltrain had to convince her that it wasn't his image he cared for, but Louise herself!

#1104 GREEN CARD WIFE—Anne Peters
Make Believe Marriage—First Comes Marriage

Silka Katarina Olsen gladly agreed to a platonic marriage with Ted Carstairs—it would allow her to work in the States and gain her citizenship. But soon Silka found herself with unfamiliar feelings for Ted that made their convenient arrangement very complicated!

#1105 ALMOST A HUSBAND—Carol Grace
Make Believe Marriage

Carrie Stephens was tired of big-city life with its big problems. She wanted to escape it, and a hopeless passion for her partner, Matt Graham. But when Matt posed as her fiancé for her new job, Carrie doubted if distance would ever make her truly forget how she loved him....

#1106 DREAM BRIDE—Terri Lindsey
Make Believe Marriage

Gloria Hamilton would only marry a man who cared for *her,* not just her sophisticated ways. So when Luke Cahill trumpeted about his qualifications for the perfect bride, Gloria decided to give Luke some lessons of her own...in love!

#1107 THE GROOM MAKER—Lisa Kaye Laurel
Make Believe Marriage

Rae Browning had lots of dates—they just ended up marrying someone else! So when sworn bachelor Trent Colton bet that she couldn't turn him into a groom, Rae knew she had a sure deal. The problem was, the only person she wanted Trent to marry was herself!

MILLION DOLLAR SWEEPSTAKES (III)

No purchase necessary. To enter, follow the directions published. Method of entry may vary. For eligibility, entries must be received no later than March 31, 1996. No liability is assumed for printing errors, lost, late or misdirected entries. Odds of winning are determined by the number of eligible entries distributed and received. Prizewinners will be determined no later than June 30, 1996.

Sweepstakes open to residents of the U.S. (except Puerto Rico), Canada, Europe and Taiwan who are 18 years of age or older. All applicable laws and regulations apply. Sweepstakes offer void wherever prohibited by law. Values of all prizes are in U.S. currency. This sweepstakes is presented by Torstar Corp., its subsidiaries and affiliates, in conjunction with book, merchandise and/or product offerings. For a copy of the Official Rules send a self-addressed, stamped envelope (WA residents need not affix return postage) to: MILLION DOLLAR SWEEPSTAKES (III) Rules, P.O. Box 4573, Blair, NE 68009, USA.

EXTRA BONUS PRIZE DRAWING

No purchase necessary. The Extra Bonus Prize will be awarded in a random drawing to be conducted no later than 5/30/96 from among all entries received. To qualify, entries must be received by 3/31/96 and comply with published directions. Drawing open to residents of the U.S. (except Puerto Rico), Canada, Europe and Taiwan who are 18 years of age or older. All applicable laws and regulations apply; offer void wherever prohibited by law. Odds of winning are dependent upon number of eligibile entries received. Prize is valued in U.S. currency. The offer is presented by Torstar Corp., its subsidiaries and affiliates in conjunction with book, merchandise and/or product offering. For a copy of the Official Rules governing this sweepstakes, send a self-addressed, stamped envelope (WA residents need not affix return postage) to: Extra Bonus Prize Drawing Rules, P.O. Box 4590, Blair, NE 68009, USA.

SWP-S895

Tall, dark and...dangerous...

Strangers in the Night

Just in time for the exciting Halloween season,
Silhouette brings you three spooky love stories in this
fabulous collection. You will love these original stories
that combine sensual romance with just a taste of
danger. Brought to you by these fabulous authors:

Anne Stuart

Chelsea Quinn Yarbro

Maggie Shayne

Available in October at a store near you.

Only from

Silhouette®

™

—where passion lives.

SHAD95

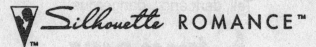

Silhouette ROMANCE™

is proud to present

The spirit of the West—and the magic of romance! Saddle up and get ready to fall in love Western-style with the fourth installment of WRANGLERS & LACE. Available in August with:

Cowboy for Hire
by Dorsey Kelley

Benton Murray was a cowboy with secrets—and now the former rodeo hero only wanted to forget the past. Then spirited Kate Monahan came to him with big plans for her own championship. All she wanted was someone to rein in her natural talent. And soon Benton was finding it difficult to deny her the help she needed—or the passion he felt for her!

Wranglers & Lace: Hard to tame—impossible to resist—these cowboys meet their match.

SL-4

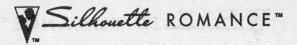

Silhouette ROMANCE™

Silhouette Romance is proud to present a new series by
Anne Peters

first Comes Marriage

GREEN CARD WIFE
Anne Peters

Sika Olsen knew her marriage to Ted Carstairs was in name only.
She would get a green card, Ted would get a substantial fee and
both of them would be happy. Until Silka found herself wishing their
arrangement could be more than just a "paper" marriage.

First Comes Marriage…will love follow?
Starting in September 1995.

FCM-1

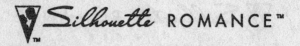

Silhouette ROMANCE™

Silhouette Romance presents the latest of Diana Palmer's much-loved series

Long Tall Texans

COLTRAIN'S PROPOSAL
DIANA PALMER

Louise Blakely was about to leave town when Jebediah Coltrain made a startling proposal—a fake engagement to save his reputation! But soon Louise suspected that the handsome doctor had more on his mind than his image. Could Jeb want Louise for life?

Coming in September from Silhouette Romance. Look for this book in our "Make-Believe Marriage" promotion.

DPLTT

As a *Privileged Woman,* you'll be entitled to all these *Free Benefits.* And *Free Gifts,* too.

To thank you for buying our books, we've designed an exclusive FREE program called *PAGES & PRIVILEGES™*. You can enroll with just one Proof of Purchase, and get the kind of luxuries that, until now, you could only read about.

Big HOTEL DISCOUNTS

A privileged woman stays in the finest hotels. And so can you—at up to 60% off! Imagine standing in a hotel check-in line and watching as the guest in front of you pays $150 for the same room that's only costing you $60. Your *Pages & Privileges* discounts are good at Sheraton, Marriott, Best Western, Hyatt and thousands of other fine hotels all over the U.S., Canada and Europe.

Free DISCOUNT TRAVEL SERVICE

A privileged woman is always jetting to romantic places. When you fly, just make one phone call for the lowest published airfare at time of booking—or double the difference back! PLUS—

you'll get a $25 voucher to use the first time you book a flight AND 5% cash back on every ticket you buy thereafter through the travel service!

SR-PP4A

$\mathcal{F}$REE GIFTS!

A privileged woman is always getting wonderful gifts.
Luxuriate in rich fragrances that will stir your senses (and his). This gift-boxed assortment of fine perfumes includes three popular scents, each in a beautiful designer bottle. Truly Lace...This luxurious fragrance unveils your sensuous side. L'Effleur...discover the romance of the Victorian era with this soft floral. Muguet des bois...a single note floral of singular beauty.

YOURS FREE!

$50 VALUE

$\mathcal{F}$REE INSIDER TIPS LETTER

A privileged woman is always informed. And you'll be, too, with our free letter full of fascinating information and sneak previews of upcoming books.

$\mathcal{M}$ORE GREAT GIFTS & BENEFITS TO COME

A privileged woman always has a lot to look forward to. And so will you. You get all these wonderful FREE gifts and benefits now with only one purchase...and there are no additional purchases required. However, each additional retail purchase of Harlequin and Silhouette books brings you a step closer to even more great FREE benefits like half-price movie tickets... and even more FREE gifts.

L'Effleur...This basketful of romance lets you discover L'Effleur from head to toe, heart to home.

Truly Lace... A basket spun with the sensuous luxuries of Truly Lace, including Dusting Powder in a reusable satin and lace covered box.

Complete the Enrollment Form in the front of this book and mail it with this Proof of Purchase.

PROOF OF PURCHASE

Pages & Privileges

Offer expires October 31, 1996

SR-PP4